T0249257

THE
BLOODLESS
PRINCES

THE
BLOODLESS
PRINCES

CHARLOTTE BOND

TOR PUBLISHING GROUP
NEW YORK

THE BLOODLESS PRINCES

A Tordotcom Book
Published by Tom Doherty Associates / Tor Publishing Group
120 Broadway
New York, NY 10271

www.torpublishinggroup.com

Tor® is a registered trademark of Macmillan Publishing Group, LLC.

The Library of Congress Cataloging-in-Publication Data is available upon request.

ISBN 978-1-250-29077-9 (hardback)
ISBN 978-1-250-29078-6 (ebook)

Our books may be purchased in bulk for promotional, educational, or business use. Please contact your local bookseller or the Macmillan Corporate and Premium Sales Department at 1-800-221-7945, extension 5442, or by email at MacmillanSpecialMarkets@macmillan.com.

First Edition: 2024

Printed in the United States of America

0 9 8 7 6 5 4 3 2 1

To Lee

*For giving wings to my words
and words to my dragons*

ONE

THE CREATION OF THE DRAGONS
The Tales of Tertian

When the universe was young and dark, light existed inside an egg. Within that egg was the whole world: land, sea, sky, dragons, and birds. Everything inside the egg had been given life by Voice, who spoke words of power to summon everything into existence.

For many generations, the world was prosperous and peaceful. But on the outside of the egg, small creatures began to crawl and tap and burrow. They swarmed over the shell, trying to get in to unlock its secrets. The dragons were unaware, but Voice knew. The creatures were scared of the dark, and Voice took pity on them.

There is enough world in here for everyone, Voice said, and because every word it spoke was true, this became true. Holes opened up in the shell, and the creatures crawled through. The dragons tried to welcome them because they were small and pink and fragile—they had no scales to protect them like the great dragons did.

These new creatures could not subsist on words and magic as the dragons did; they needed the waters in the rivers and the produce of the land. Even then, they were still starving, so Voice spoke into being heavy-beasts and earth-clouds, pink-squealers and hairy-screamers. When Voice saw how much the egg-crackers valued these animals, it also spoke into being all other creatures in the world: moon-howlers and earth-lumberers, slither-cousins and web-weavers, pond-leapers and more feathered-fellows, heather-steppers and ground-skitters. Soon, the world was crawling with new creatures, but nobody minded because, as Voice had promised, the world was big enough for everyone. But the egg-crackers eventually spread so far and wide that they needed more space to grow their crops and feed their animals. They asked Voice what they should do, and Voice thought on the matter before approaching the dragons to say: *These creatures need soft earth, water, and the sun to live their lives, but you do not. Are you willing to live beneath the earth or on top of hills or mountains where these creatures cannot farm?*

The dragons were a little hesitant because while they could see the truth of this, they also loved the fields and sky and wide-open spaces. Seeing their reluctance, Voice spoke words of beauty, and the rocks of the world filled up with earth-ribbons and stone-eyes.

There, said Voice. *Now the inside of the world is beautiful too. Will it make a pleasing home for you?* The dragons agreed it would, having instantly fallen in love with the earth-ribbons and stone-eyes. And so they moved into the heart of the earth, digging themselves caves and tunnels, that sparkled and shone.

This story was told to me by P'tarmia and Clarix. Both dragons agreed that a lot of hardship might have been avoided if the dirt-walkers had left the deep-dwellers alone and, in particular, if they had not gone after the earth-ribbons and stone-eyes.

On a personal note, I find it fascinating that in the dragon creation myth, the birds were created at the same time as dragons, whereas humans and all land-grubbers were made later. I have often thought there might be a link between dragons and birds—especially with eye colour. Dragons exhibit the same pigmentation as owls—namely, nocturnal dragons have black eyes; diurnal, blue; and crepuscular, orange, thus reflecting the colour of the sky. It would be a fascinating field of study to see whether dragons have more in common with birds than snakes (many of my mage brothers currently believe snakes are close cousins to dragons), but I believe no one outside of myself is interested in such matters, so the likelihood of further study is minimal, especially since I suspect the Mage Guild will simply burn my manuscript upon receiving it.

HOW THE WORLD WAS MADE
Troubadour Tales

The universe was black and empty, except for two stars. These stars existed for many years before changing their form to become the Allmother and Allfather.

With these new forms, the gods wanted a new place to live and so created the world. First, they created night and day, then land and sea. The Allfather loved the openness of the sky and the wide expanse of the sea, so he took dominion over those; the Allmother liked the solidness of the soil beneath her feet and its quiet spaces, so she took dominion over those.

Each day, one of them created something new for the world. The Allmother created all the things that walked on the ground and lived in it, while the Allfather created all creatures that fly or swim.

There were only two creatures that the Allmother and Allfather made together. First, the butterfly. A creature of the earth, then of the air. Thus it is unique among all creatures and can travel through all known realms.

Second, they made men and women; the Allmother created their bodies from the earth while the Allfather filled their bodies with breath. These humans were to care for the earth while the Allmother and Allfather continued to create many more creatures.

"Swear to us an oath that you will always watch over these lands and care for the animals we give you," the Allfather said.

Falling to their knees, the first men and women replied joyfully, "We swear," and so the First Oath was born. Since then, all oaths of importance have been sworn to the Allfather.

The gods were very pleased with their creations, but when the Allmother created the elephant, the Allfather grew jealous, for he had created no beast that could rival it.

"But you have the whales of the sea," the Allmother soothed, "and they are far bigger than my elephants."

"But they are hidden away," the Allfather opined. "No one can see their majesty. I wish to create something to soar through the sky, that I can ride the way the humans ride elephants."

So the Allfather created the dragon. To bear him, it had to withstand his godliness, so he imbued it with magic and made it of a great size—as large as a cloud—to equal his own majesty. It had to be greater than all the beasts of the world, so he combined many of their elements: scales to glide through the air like fish swim through water, feathers to soar through the skies, whiskers to sense every air current, and horns to inspire awe and dread in all who looked upon it.

The Allfather was impressed by this truly magnificent beast he had made. But the Allmother, who can see into the heart of all things, saw that the dragon was proud—too proud to do as the Allfather wished and bear him on its back. The Allmother was proved right.

All the creatures of the world held the dragon in dread esteem, and so it did nothing but preen itself and strut about and listened not to its creator. The Allfather, incensed at the dragon's refusal to do his bidding, flung the great beast to the top of the highest mountain, far from its fawning admirers.

The dragon raged, then sulked before an idea for revenge came to it. Curling itself around the mountain several times, the dragon cut off all the rivers and streams that ran down into the world.

Humans and animals alike began to sicken and die. With the Allfather in a furious temper and the Allmother busy soothing him, the humans dared not ask for divine help. Instead, they sent their best champions to destroy the dragon. But the beast wrapped its great coils around each and squeezed the life from them.

After many men had died this way, the wisest humans cautiously approached the Allmother, who advised that fourteen men should be decked in spike-covered armour and sent up the mountain on elephants, similarly protected. While the humans forged the armour, the Allmother struck the ground at the base of the mountain, letting out some of the trapped water so that no more creatures might die.

When the dragon saw what she had done, it clamped its mouth over the greatest of the springs and started to drink the water away. The Allmother's stream dried up, but the god whispered to the water to find new ways to trickle through the mountain, and so it did.

When the fourteen champions and their mounts were ready, they started up the mountain, and when the dragon saw the new champions, it laughed.

"I have crushed over a hundred of your predecessors; another fourteen will be easy. I have not tasted elephant flesh, but I shall hang it in the dark caves of my mountain until it is sweet and rotting."

With that, the dragon unfurled itself and slithered towards its challengers, wrapping its lengthy body around all of them at once. Then it squeezed.

When the armoured spikes pierced its flesh, the creature bled, shrieked, shifted its grip, and squeezed again. This time, the spikes punctured its bones. Again the dragon shifted, but this time, its innards were pierced and, full of the water it had drunk, they burst. Its skin split apart, and water gushed out, carrying away its entrails. The dragon screamed as it died, and that scream became the gales that rage around the earth on dark nights. The dragon's blood soaked into the mountain, turning the stone itself red. And its guts, as they slithered down the mountainside, became new dragons—but smaller and afraid of this new world they found themselves in.

The blood-soaked champions were proclaimed the first kings of the fourteen realms. The elephants were set loose, never to work again and only to enjoy a life of peace.

Many called for the new dragons to be killed, lest they grow up like their progenitor. But the Allfather stepped forward and said mercy would be given. "These dragons are blameless, and they will be allowed to live. With the Allmother's permission, they will be given homes in the earth itself. They may fly but intermittently. Mostly, they must keep to their new caves. Will you give them a beautiful home?" he beseeched his fellow god.

The Allmother carved out caves in the mountains and hills across the world, filling them with gold and gems to make them beautiful, and there the dragons dwelt.

TWO

Maddileh looked around her with wonder. Every time she came here, she noticed something different. The first time, she'd realised just how high the ceilings were, something she'd only noticed in passing when she'd been in the cave with Petros. Later, she'd seen they were vaulted and carved. It was amazing what you could observe without the threat of bone-blistering fire engulfing you. And how often did anyone get to linger in a dragon's lair?

At first, she'd thought she was dreaming, reliving her quest. But her dreams were usually a confused mixture of action and emotions. These visits to the White Lady's lair were calm and, upon waking, perfectly recollectable. There were details here that her mind couldn't have made up, like the carvings on the pillars. Presumably, they went all the way from floor to ceiling, but she could only vouch for as far as she could see. At first, she'd thought them merely a pattern, but now she thought they looked more like an in-decipherable language of curls and dots.

Saralene would know what these are. Maddileh had been tempted more than once to mention her dreams to the High Mage and obtain advice. But before Maddileh said any-thing, she wanted to make sure this wasn't something sinis-ter. After all, Petros had died in the White Lady's tunnels, so perhaps this was an illusion masking a trap. What if he was dangling the mystery in front of her to tempt her to bring Saralene here to get revenge on them both? Maddileh knew that if she told Saralene about this dream and the High Mage decided to investigate, there would be no stopping her. So, for now, she kept her peace and merely tried to observe all she could.

Squinting upwards, Maddileh thought she could make out statues on distant ledges, but it was too dark to be sure. The dragon-bile flames were dwindling, and without any dragon to vomit up new ones, the lair was a little darker each time.

Allfather save us—what if I keep coming here when it's truly dark? The thought sent a shudder through her. This place was undeniably impressive, with its surprisingly elaborate architecture and glittering piles of treasure (which included—because it was collected by a dragon—bits of broken glass, nails, and roof tiles as well as gold and gems). But if the dancing shadows around her swallowed the whole cavern, Maddileh could imagine that the empty space would become malevolent and full of creeping unseen horrors.

Made uneasy by her own imaginings, Maddileh headed towards the spot that always drew her. She felt certain that one day, she would turn the corner and find the White Lady gone from her resting place, and she wasn't sure how she'd feel about such a discovery.

Dragon hunters fell into one of two categories: heroic or stupid. On the moment of its death, a dragon's magic would deliver one final, deadly defensive strike—an explosion that brought the ceiling down, a burst of acid slime that ate through armour, or perhaps a foul vapour that would seep into your eyes, ears, and nose, trapping you in darkness forever. Naturally, every dragon hunter believed they were the heroic sort, and only evidence recorded in the mage orbs held in the Mage Museum or the stories written down in *The Demise and Demesne of Dragons* revealed the truth. When she'd set out on her quest for the Fireborne Blade, Maddileh had been sure she'd been heroic too. She'd certainly succeeded and survived—a usual requirement for heroism. She was also now the High Mage's Champion, a post created especially for her. Many of those knights who had sneered at her when she was the newly made Knight of the Stairs now treated her with deference and even a little awe. Of course, there were still plenty who bowed when she faced them and belittled her the moment her back was turned, but at least they were in the minority these days.

But as she lay in bed at night, thoughts plagued her that the Blade and her place in the world had come at too high a cost. She'd never encountered a dragon like the White Lady before. In fact, she'd only encountered one dragon directly— the Shimmering Corsair. He had been a ball of fierce, fiery fury to be dispatched as quickly as possible. She'd had no qualms when her master, Sir Osbert, had finished the beast off. But facing the White Lady had been different because the dragon had spoken to her. Dragons were supposed to be vermin that plagued the land, stealing sheep, cattle, and valuables. But the White Lady had been graceful and eloquent. When her golden eyes had peered at Maddileh and Saralene, the knight had felt a flash of humiliation, similar to when her mother had inspected her attire on a morning; she'd been assessed and found wanting. This wasn't a creature that acted on instinct alone, one that was ruled by its belly and its greed. And now it seemed, the dragon lived in a cave that spoke of craftsmanship and refinement. What was to be made of that?

Maddileh had scoured every volume of *The Demise and Demesne of Dragons* for mentions of dragons speaking; there were none. It was hinted at in stories and fables, such as those found in *Troubadour Tales*, but no knight had ever reported back to the investigating mages that a dragon had spoken to them.

Yet the lack of such information meant little; after all, Maddileh hadn't told the mages about her own experience, so what was to say that other knights hadn't either? A creature that talked was an intelligent creature, higher than vermin, and one that should not be sought out and destroyed in the way knights of the fourteen realms hunted dragons.

No matter how many times she eroded her doubts about killing a creature that didn't deserve to be killed, the thoughts kept worming their way back in. There was, of course, someone who knew more about dragons than any investigative mage and who might be able to help her, but that would mean going home, something Maddileh had sworn never to do.

Maddileh turned a corner, and there was the White Lady, her skin glittering with frost. Now that the cavern was growing gloomier, it was apparent that the White Lady was giving off her own subtle glow, making the gems sparkle. The beauty of it made Maddileh smile.

Smiling at raven-fodder, are we? came the voice from the cave. *I should expect no less from a gem-stealer.*

"I keep telling you"—Maddileh's voice seemed painfully loud in the silent cave and she lowered it to a whisper—"I'm not here to steal anything. I don't even *want* to be here. I don't know *why* I'm here. Did *you* bring me here?"

I? No. You brought yourself.

Maddileh gritted her teeth. The unidentified voice always gave an answer that was unsatisfactory and vague. It had a feminine tone, but that meant nothing; it could still be part of a trick.

"Tell me who you are. Are you . . . Petros?" That name fell heavy and dead in the silence.

You fear that name, the voice mused.

"Fear? No. Mistrust? Absolutely. He killed me, then I killed him, so we should be even, but he doesn't strike me as someone who lets things lie—especially not his own bones." Some distance away, there was the tinkle of disturbed treasure sliding to the floor. Instinctively, Maddileh's hand went to her belt, but there was no sword there. There never was, even when she fell asleep clutching one tightly.

"Who are you?" she said, her voice low and urgent.

I am cold, came the reply, and Maddileh woke up. In a moment of chilly clarity, she was almost certain she knew who was speaking to her, and the knowledge brought no comfort.

Maddileh stared at the open copy of *The Demise and Demesne of Dragons* in front of her.

I've been an utter fool. Why didn't I read this before? I yearned all my life to have my name in one of these volumes, and when it was added, I didn't read it. She knew why, of course: because she'd been ashamed of herself, and angry for being ashamed. It was shameful to kill a noble creature—and if dragons were noble, that meant the history of knights and Maddileh's whole life was based on cruelty.

Now her gaze drifted back down to the book:

By order of the emperor, in consultation with the High Mage, a delegation of mages and warriors set out to the demesne of the White Lady.

Unlike other lairs of dead dragons, the tunnels still showed signs of recent soot drake activity. Furthermore, the delegation encountered no less than five dragon-dead. Previous records indicate that such creatures are not usually found in a lair more than six months to a year after the dragon's demise (although see the Silken Sigh, the Ancient Terror, and the Deadly Wyrm for notable exceptions).

When the delegation reached the heart of the lair, they reported that the White Lady was still corporeal. Her corpse had not decayed or destroyed itself in the manner of all other dragons on record, but was whole and covered in frost. The spear that the Mage's Champion used to fell the beast still protruded from the creature's mouth; blood was crusted upon it. After careful examination, it was declared that the White Lady was not breathing, nor did she have a heart-beat. Yet despite lacking vital signs, the dragon was seen to twitch her claws, much like a dog will twitch its leg while dreaming. All but two of the eight-strong party witnessed this.

After much discussion, it was held that the White Lady was not dead but merely held in some deep—possibly magical—sleep. It is beyond our skill to say whether the sleep was instigated by the weapon or an act of self-preservation by the dragon herself, whether the sleep will end, or what it is that she dreams about.

She isn't dead. She's dreaming. I should have read this before. Stupid woman. Stupid.

Never mind. What's done is done. Concentrate on what to do next. I need to find out if she's in my dreams or if I'm in hers— and how I stop them.

It had been almost three years since Maddileh had ventured—unknowingly, for the second time—into the demesne of the White Lady; three years since both she and Saralene had perished and come back; three years of maintaining their positions of power in the Citadel of the Mages. During that time, Maddileh had agonised over her killing blow of the White Lady. Now that it appeared the blow hadn't been killing at all, a dark shadow lifted as if she'd finally voided herself of a wriggling in her guts.

Of course, while her death-guilt might have lifted, she now had to deal with the concept that dragons might be more than everyone thought and what that might mean for their world.

I need to talk to the White Lady herself. See what kind of creature she truly is.

With this decision made, relief flooded through her; this was a *mage's* problem as much as it was a knight's, and it meant that Maddileh could tell Saralene. Putting on a jerkin and trousers, the Blade and a dagger at her belt, she stepped out of the library.

Despite it being the early hours of the morning, Maddileh had no qualms about seeking out the High Mage. Her friend worked day and night, sleeping when her body demanded rest rather than on a schedule. It had seemed to work well at first, with Saralene looking rejuvenated and alert whenever she appeared. But in the last few months, Maddileh had started to notice little signs of strain: a tension around the mouth, moments of distracted listlessness where Saralene would gaze vacantly into the distance. Such unguarded moments never happened when Saralene was with other mages, citizens, or the emperor's officials; then, she was as sharp-witted and composed as ever. Only when she was with Maddileh did her mask of composure slip. Such honesty and vulnerability between them made Maddileh's heart both glow and ache.

Walking through the High Mage's palace, Maddileh let the solitude wash over her. She had been amazed to see that the palaces of both the High Mage and the emperor had impossibly high ceilings. *Who could need so much space above their heads?* Maddileh had wondered as she'd walked the hallways for the first time. It wasn't as if the walls were hung with a wealth of tapestries and pictures. Apparently, there had once been a twenty-foot-high portrait of a former ruler at the emperor's palace, but it had been chopped off the wall by revolutionaries and used on the pyre they'd erected to burn said emperor. After that, all subsequent rulers had avoided such grandiose gestures out of a persistent sense of superstition.

After the initial strangeness dissipated, Maddileh had grown to like how her footsteps rang and echoed in the corridor, as if she was striding out on important business.

Rain rattled against the towering windows, adding another layer of peacefulness to the place.

As much as she liked the grand corridors, Maddileh couldn't have slept beneath such a vast space, and her private apartments next to Saralene's had ceilings of normal height. Nevertheless, the floor plan of her private rooms was equal to three rooms at Fort Helm, where she'd grown up, far more space than Maddileh was used to. She felt like a crab in a shell far too big for it.

When Maddileh reached Saralene's door, she knocked and called out, "Saralene?" There was no answer but instead the sound of a table shifting suddenly, its legs screeching on tile. "Saralene?" she called more urgently, her hand already on the handle. A wheezing gasp from inside had her throwing open the door and charging in. There was a figure in the room, sagging against the great bed; it wore Saralene's clothes, but it was not she. Hosh, the previous High Mage who'd fought death for over a century and had ultimately been displaced by Saralene's spell, was half-sprawled on the bed, his wizened hand clutching his chest, his bloody mouth grinning as he stared at her.

"So, it's you," he said, his voice hoarse and cracked. "You'll be the first one I shall kill." He tried to get to his feet, but Saralene's skirts caught under his heels so that he fell back again.

Instantly, Maddileh was on him, her dagger at his throat, her other hand pinning him down. "Where is she?" she hissed. "You maggot—what have you done? I'll kill you."

"No, I'll kill—" Hosh's voice became thick and phlegmy; his face contorted in pain. There was a sickening crunch, and the man's skin shifted, stretching in some places, shrinking in others. In the space of a few heartbeats, it was not Hosh beneath her but Saralene looking disoriented and sick.

"Maddileh—it's me. Saralene. Please, whatever you think you saw, don't be hasty."

The pain that had been building behind Saralene's eyes all day had spread through her head, down her neck, across her shoulders, and gradually crept all the way down to her shins. There wasn't a bit of her that didn't hurt. There were no tender spots, no sore muscles, just a bone-deep ache that she put down to exhaustion, causing her to retire early. The discomfort didn't get any better with rest, but it didn't get any worse either, and she lay on her couch in her loosest dress to ensure no boning or stitching pressed against her. Her gaze rested on the glowing embers of the fire, and she was soothed by the hiss of raindrops falling down the chimney. Gradually, her eyes closed, and she imagined herself back in the nursery with her two younger sisters. When Petros had moved out of the nursery into rooms of his own, all three Silverlock girls had rested easier in their beds: no vicious pinchings as wake-up calls, no chance of finding pondweed under the blankets, no sand sprinkled on pillows so that it got into hair, ears, and teeth for days after.

As the eldest of Lord Silverlock's second wife, Saralene should have been moved to her own rooms first, but as with everything in the house, Petros had gotten precedence and been given rooms that should have been hers. For once, Saralene had not minded. It was comforting to hear other breaths in the room when she woke at night, and when one of the girls suffered some injustice that left their backsides smarting and Petros smirking, the nursery was where they went to soothe their hurts and tell stories of princesses, mages, and knights who forged their own destinies.

Older now, and filled with the cares of a High Mage, Saralene was grateful for the peace of her own rooms; she'd even banned the palace maids from entering without her express permission. Nevertheless, she was also grateful that Maddileh had taken the adjoining rooms. In truth, Saralene had been trying to think of a way to put that very arrangement to her Champion when they were shown potential rooms. But Maddileh had taken the tour, seen all the rooms, then walked back to those adjoining the High Mage's apartment and said, "These ones."

Some nights, Saralene lay in bed and wondered what it would be like to have the knight not in a bed next door but in her own bed, their limbs sleepily entangled. Maddileh could be frustratingly unreadable when she chose, and Saralene could just imagine the knight's face going calm and smooth the way it did when she was hiding her emotions, and Saralene would never know if her request had been turned down due to distaste or indifference or something else.

All this magic I command, and I can't tell if the woman I love loves me.

As Saralene slipped towards sleep, the crackle of the fire turned to another sound: the distinctive whistle of soft wind through long grass. She opened her eyes and found herself lying not on the couch but on a garden lawn. Beyond the boundary wall was a gently swaying sea of green grass. Saralene sat bolt upright, an exclamation of shock trapped in her throat. Around her bloomed roses, harebells, magnolias, and cowslips—except they all looked slightly askew. The cowslips short and stumpy, the roses so large that their heads bent heavily with petals falling onto the grass. A gust of wind brought her the unmistakable perfume of the magnolia trees intertwined with a scent of wet earth that stuck in the nose.

From somewhere unseen came the babble of a stream. Behind her was a house—a spacious one with sharp lines contrasting against a thatched roof. The front door opened, and a woman stepped out, wiping her hands on a dishcloth, yet this was clearly no maid. She had fine dark skin which shimmered as if shards of moonlight had settled there. Her lips were the deep red of ripe cherries, and her brown eyes sparkled. The slenderness of her form was enhanced by hair that reached her waist, braided down almost to the tips, where gold beads had been woven into the strands. She had all the marks of a fine lady yet carried a dishcloth, had a smear of flour on her cheek, and what was either dirt or soot marking her apron. She walked down the garden path, evidently more curious than perturbed at finding someone there.

"Well, you are looking different today. I hope it puts you in a better temper."

Saralene looked around, certain that the woman must be addressing someone else, but there were just the two of them in the garden. "I'm . . . sorry?" Saralene said, a thousand questions running through her head too fast for her to snatch at one. The woman narrowed her eyes.

"You're not him, are you?"

"Who?"

"The wizened one. Irritable. Raging. Sulking. Smug. If you've come to take his place, then I can't say I'm disappointed in the loss of his company. However, I would like to know how and why you've both turned up here."

"Where is here?" Saralene asked.

The woman gave her a strange smile. "Ah. I see. You don't know. Well, look over there, and perhaps you'll be able to guess." She pointed beyond the garden wall, and the impossibility of the sight twisted Saralene's guts like a vice. The field of grass flowed down to a distant road that ran past the house. To the left, the road led to a bridge that had been crafted from one long solid stretch of rock, its jagged sides making it appear grown rather than hewn. What was on the other side of the bridge was impossible to see due to the dark shadows gathered there, but legend told her what lay beyond: the world of the living.

"Where is she?" The voice was low, furious, disgusted, but Saralene would recognise it anywhere.

"Maddileh?" She turned, searching frantically. There was both despair and comfort at the thought of her best friend being in the Gravelands with her.

"You maggot—what have you done?"

Facing away from the bridge now, Saralene's attention was divided between the great, sprawling city in the distance and the wall of her chambers, which seemed as if it lay at the end of a tunnel. A terrible memory, repressed for three years, came to the forefront of her mind: traveling down such a tunnel, feeling her body squeezed like an apple in a press, sensing the withered Hosh hurtling in the opposite direction, his shrieks of terror so sharp they sliced into her skull. And now this memory became a reality, and she was no longer in the garden but hurtling back into her body. There was a moment when everything was filled with pain, but that was a blessed relief because such sensations meant she was alive and out of the Gravelands. Then came the feel of a knife at her throat, bringing with it the very real fear that she might be sent back to the realms of the dead.

"Maddileh—it's me. Saralene," she said, her voice hoarse. "Please, whatever you think you saw, don't be hasty."

THREE

LEGENDS OF THE FOURTEEN REALMS

Once there was a queen of the Third Realm who was the wisest of all women. Her subjects loved her and would take their grievances to her, certain of a fair resolution. When standing in judgment, Luciel would always have with her the lightning oak staff—a symbol of her queenship. Legend has it that at the moment of her birth, the ground shook and lightning arced down from a clear sky and split in half a mighty oak. When she took up her crown, Luciel had a branch hewn off the lightning-struck oak, which she said connected her to the wisdom of both the Allmother and the Allfather.

Certainly, this queen had the same ability as the Allmother to see into the hearts of men and women, enabling her to make fair judgments on all who came before her. Yet with such great wisdom, Luciel never found a man or woman with whom she could fall in love. Her ability to see into the hearts of those around her meant that she could never ignore the flaws of the people she met.

Furthermore, she was wary that her reputation for good counsel would be marred by anyone she married. As consort, they would be called on to make their own judgments on certain matters, and since they would naturally err, Luciel's reputation would be tarnished.

Then, one day, she had cause to seek counsel herself—from the Allfather, since how to resolve a drought was beyond her wisdom. At that time, the gods were beginning to withdraw from humankind, but they still occasionally walked the world, so when the Allfather heard Luciel's pleas for help, he attended her, curious to meet the woman who held such sway over the Third Realm. It took only one of Luciel's heartbeats for both of them to fall in love.

They met often after that, finding wisdom in each other's words, comfort in each other's presence; their flaws (for even a god has flaws) mattered not at all.

The Allfather declared to his fellow god that he would wed Luciel and they would live in the sky together. The Allmother gently reminded him that since Luciel was human, living in the sky would take a lot of magic.

"What of it?" declared the Allfather. "I have all the magic in the world at my disposal."

Seeing that she could get nowhere with the Allfather, the Allmother instead approached Luciel. "Look into my heart, Luciel, and see how joyful I am that you and the Allfather have found each other." Luciel did so. "Know then that my words are not from jealousy but from love for you both: You cannot marry him as you are. I made you from the clay of the world. If I could give you up to the Allfather, I would. But I cannot. He believes magic will change you, and it will. You can live with him as he foresees and rule beside him, but the you doing this would not be the you who stands before me. Magic changes what it touches, and it will change you. Your soul, your wisdom, your compassion, and your reason would be altered."

Tears poured down Luciel's face, for she saw the truth in

the Allmother's words. "Then I must live alone and never with the one whom I love."

"The former is certainly true, but the latter may not be. There is a way for you to be with the Allfather, but you would need to live alone until then, and you would need to live a very long time.

"What I propose is as follows: the Bloodless Princes who rule the Gravelands cannot decide on who should enter which realm. They argue over every soul, and so the dead linger, displaced and unsettled. There is a bridge leading from our world to theirs, named the Perilous Bridge, for it spans a great chasm. I will install you on this bridge, and you shall judge the souls that enter the Gravelands. Those destined for the Sunrise Prince's realm—those of purest heart—you shall allow to pass. Those with wicked souls, you shall cast from the bridge into the realm of the Sunset Prince.

"If you judge the dead until time runs out, the world will be flooded with magic so that all is transformed. It will be a magic made from both the Allfather's power and mine, so it will burn away the body I have gifted you, and your soul will be free to marry him, unchanged and wholly yourself."

Luciel wept then, both for joy and sorrow. For the end of the world was very far away, and she would have to wait a long, long time for the one whom she loved. Yet she could live with hope.

"I agree, and am humbled that I should be given such power and responsibility."

And so Luciel made her goodbyes, and the Allmother carried her to the Perilous Bridge to begin her tenure as its guardian.

When the Allfather found out what had been agreed, he

raged so violently that storms engulfed the world for seven days and nights. The Allmother was so alarmed by his grief that she sent a butterfly guard to conduct Luciel from the Gravelands to the realm of the Allfather, where she dried his tears, kissed his brow, and told him that she would wait for him and never stop loving him. The Allfather was ashamed then of how he had acted, and he accompanied Luciel down to her new realm, where he created her a small house and garden where she might sit and wait for him in comfort. But because the stone and growing things of the earth were not within the Allfather's dominion, his attempts were mis-shapen and illogical. Luciel laughed delightedly and said, "No one in the world above or the Gravelands has such a home. I shall cherish it until the end of time sweeps it away, and I shall think of you, my love, whenever I am there."

The Allfather also set a stream running from the living world into Luciel's garden so that news of all that passed there could trickle down to her. Then he returned to his position in the sky, clearing it of clouds and bathing the land in sunshine.

And so Luciel became the Waiting Woman, the Judge, and the Guardian of the Bridge, and thus she remains to this day. Before they go into danger, men and women will say to each other: *May you walk the Bridge untroubled*, meaning that should any of them die, they will find Luciel waiting to guide them across rather than cast them down.

FOUR

"You saw the Perilous Bridge?" Maddileh said, aghast but also in awe. "What was it like?"

"Just like the stories say," Saralene replied. "One long piece of stone heading into darkness."

"And Luciel—what was she like?"

"She was beautiful. But annoyed—with Hosh, I think, who must have been there before he switched places with me. What did you see when you came into my rooms?"

Maddileh related all that had happened, although she didn't mention the reason for seeking out Saralene. A sleeping dragon talking to you in your dreams didn't seem the most important issue right now.

"What do you think happened?" Maddileh asked when she'd finished.

"I don't know." Saralene frowned at the ashes of the fire. After a pause, she looked up and asked, "Has anything like this happened to you? With Petros?"

Maddileh recoiled. "No! If it had, I'd have come straight to you. This is far beyond the remit of a knight. Although, I will, of course, help you in any way I can." Once the promise was out, she felt foolish for saying something so mawkish. But her uncertainties lifted when Saralene smiled at her with relief and gratitude.

"Thank you. I wondered . . . would you sleep in here tonight? If it happens again, I don't want palace guards coming in. And"—she bit her lower lip, looking gloriously shy—"it was actually your words that brought me back. Your voice. If it happens again, I'll need you to bring me back from the Gravelands."

Suddenly, it seemed to Maddileh that they were sitting too close, yet all she wanted to do was draw closer still. Instead, she reached out and laid a hand on Saralene's and said softly, "If I have to walk the Perilous Bridge and fight my way to Findara itself, I will always come for you." She squeezed Saralene's hand ever so gently, and Saralene squeezed back.

One of Maddileh's duties as the High Mage's Champion was to oversee the training of the palace guards. Over time, Maddileh had promoted some of the more senior guards to trainers as well, and she now handed over to them complete control of the training ground so that she could retreat to the mages' library and look through the books for any hint that might help Saralene unknit whatever curse was upon her.

The two of them fell into a routine. In the morning, Saralene would leave out a pile of books and copious amounts of torn paper to use as bookmarks. While Saralene attended essential meetings of magic and state, Maddileh would look through the books and mark pages mentioning anything from a preapproved list that included the Resurrection Bowl, death-avoidance spells, phoenix feathers, and blood magic. When Saralene was free of obligations, she would look through the marked pages, scribbling in a notebook. When Maddileh was done with Saralene's research, she continued with her own, looking for anything that mentioned talking dragons.

After several weeks, neither of them had advanced much in their studies, and Maddileh was beginning to feel dread settling into her bones. Matters weren't helped by waking up one night to find a figure limping across the bedroom towards the door; she realised only just in time that it was Hosh, and she pinned him to the wall, her hand over his mouth while she repeated Saralene's name over and over until her friend came back to her. Saralene was trembling so much that Maddileh put her to bed, then lay next to her, stroking her friend's hair until Saralene finally fell asleep. Maddileh had meant to move after that, but the bed had been comfy, and since having Saralene next to her would alert her the second the transformation happened again, she ended up staying there until she fell asleep herself. Her repeated thought of *Just a little longer and then I'll move* followed her down into slumber.

Following that night, Saralene insisted on sleeping with her wrist chained to the bedpost so that if the change happened again, there was less chance of the old man reaching the door. Saralene was careful to hide the shackle each morning after Maddileh unlocked it, but the knight couldn't shake a misgiving that one of the maids might find it, and then speculation would run rife as to what the High Mage and her Champion got up to at night, especially since it must now be known that Maddileh slept in Saralene's rooms.

It was getting to the point where Maddileh hadn't dreamed herself in the White Lady's lair for so long that she felt that perhaps the dreams were over. And then, one night, she was back there.

As she stood before the sleeping dragon, all was silent. No voice, no crackle of fire, no drip of water from the ceiling. Maddileh took a deep breath, ready to test her theory.

"White Lady—are you there?"

The voice whispered back, *Tell your heart-mate that I can help her, but you must both come to me.*

Then with a jolt, Maddileh was pushed out of the dream, back into the waking world.

FIVE

THE DEMISE AND DEMESNE OF DRAGONS
Appendix 34: The Weldrake Repository

The Weldrake Repository is held at Fort Helm under the stewardship of Lady Weldrake. There is an ancient legend (see *The Dragon in the Well*) that ties the female members of the Blackwyn family to this role.

Despite the fact that the Mage Museum is far greater and holds more significant items, a little value can be assigned to the Weldrake Repository, for it holds numerous oddities that would find no place in the Mage Museum and would otherwise be discarded.

However, scholars are advised to examine the repository's contents with a discerning eye since there is much of folklore and fairy tale there. Items that would not pass the rigorous inspections and tests required for adoption into the Mage Museum are contained therein, making the Weldrake Repository an assemblage of interesting curios rather than a serious collection.

SIX

"So, dragons can talk," Saralene said, sounding more thoughtful than surprised. "I always considered them vermin. Carrying off cattle and gold and suchlike."

They were out riding together, Saralene with a hawk on her wrist. The bird's plumage had a red tint to it, and the summer sunshine lent its glossy feathers the sheen of glowing embers. Maddileh always felt a little uncomfortable seeing how the hawk managed to keep itself steady on Saralene's wrist while the rest of her rolled side to side with the horse's gait. It didn't look natural. The High Mage herself was wearing a hunting outfit of rich brown, the skirt split for riding. Saralene only ever wore browns and deep reds. "Mother never used to let me wear these colours as a child," she'd confided once. "It was always green or yellow, like our crest. I swore if I ever broke free of them, I'd wear browns and reds forever."

Maddileh, of course, wore her usual jerkin, breeches, and boots.

"You're not alone in that opinion," Maddileh said, relieved that this awkward conversation was going better than expected. "I must have scoured most of the mages' library, and I can't find anything about them talking. Except in the old folktales, where they can talk to the smith and Livia, but nothing more recent than that. And I'd always put those stories down to whimsy."

"Based on what you've found out, then," Saralene mused, "dragons used to be able to talk but then couldn't or wouldn't. But now the White Lady is talking to you. Can anyone else hear her, do you think?"

"I don't know. Did you hear her when we were in the cave?"

"Not that I recall."

"Then maybe it's just me, or maybe you were too far away. The words don't come out of her mouth, more sort of . . . turn up in your head." Maddileh shifted in the saddle. Explained out loud, it sounded quite ridiculous. "Maybe it was just a dream."

Saralene sighed and halted the horse. "Perhaps it was, but if she says she can help me, then what choice do we have but to go and see? After all, we've been searching for weeks and found nothing. We don't know when Hosh will make his next move. We've been able to overpower him so far, but how long until something happens and I can't get back? We need to follow this up."

Saralene stroked the breast of the bird thoughtfully, and it nipped at her fingers. Maddileh frowned. "You shouldn't let it do that. It'll have one of your fingers off someday."

"You wouldn't do that, would you, Embers?" Saralene said. The hawk cocked its head and gave a little chirrup that sounded odd coming from its fearsomely curved beak. "I raised him from his egg."

"I'll never understand your obsession with birds. Dogs I can understand. They give companionship and can hunt and guard. But your birds don't do any of that. They won't lick your face, but they might scratch your eyes out." Seeing Saralene's look, she said, "All right. I admit you can hunt with them, but using a bow and arrow would be more useful and less dangerous. They're just tools, but unpredictable ones. I do not see the attraction."

Saralene loosened the jesses, then launched the hawk into the air, where it rose, found a thermal, and spiraled lazily in the sky. "But you don't like *any* animals," she said mildly. "Birds aren't as affectionate as dogs, true, but they have a raw, natural beauty that dogs gave up centuries ago in return for a belly rub. You can never truly command a hawk or falcon, only work with it. In their wildness lies their beauty and their charm."

"And their ability to rake your eyes out," Maddileh said grimly.

Saralene smiled, and their conversation was replaced by the sough of the wind through the trees and the distant call of the hawk.

"When we go to see the dragon," Saralene continued eventually, "we need to be prepared."

"Yes. I've made an inventory of the armoury both here and at—" Maddileh was cut short by a snort of laughter.

"I'm sorry," Saralene said. "I forget sometimes just how different our disciplines are. I meant we should find out as much as we can about the dragon before we go. Why didn't the spear kill it? How can we communicate with it safely?"

Maddileh deliberately looked away, wanting to distance herself from where the conversation was going.

"I'm not suggesting we visit the Weldrake Repository," Saralene added hastily. "I would never ask you to go home when you didn't want to. But perhaps we could write to your aunt and seek her counsel."

Maddileh forced her stiffened shoulders to relax. For all

their friendship, Saralene was the High Mage, and if she insisted they travel to Fort Helm, her Champion would have been obliged to do so. But Saralene was offering a compromise.

"That sounds wise," Maddileh said. "Can you enchant the missive you send? My father . . . does not have an easy relationship with my aunt. If he intercepts the letter, he will no doubt interfere, maybe even take over, and I wouldn't trust him to know one end of a book from his arsehole."

Saralene snorted again, covering her mouth with her hand in a belated attempt to look ladylike. "Noted."

"Oh, and send Aunt Wren some of that Linna gingerbread we have in the kitchens. She loves that, and Lord Blackwyn never buys it." Maddileh grinned, her spirits lifting. "With secret messages he can't read and gingerbread he won't buy, he's going to be furious. I feel quite cheered up."

Given how swiftly the books arrived, Maddileh was certain that Saralene had used some kind of magic to transmit messages.

"Only to get the message to Lady Weldrake," Saralene said when Maddileh asked. "I wouldn't dare send such valuable books as these via magical methods. It's highly unlikely that anything would go wrong, but any risk is too much." With a sly smile, she added, "So I simply included a message to your father saying that the books were imperative for my research and that he should send a company of armed guards with them. I thought you'd approve of the inconvenience."

Maddileh grinned. "Very much so."

Saralene had a meeting with the emperor that morning that could not be postponed, and so Maddileh sat down in their private apartments to read what her aunt had sent. There was a covering note.

> *Your Greatness, and my dear niece,*
>
> *I enclose for your attention the books I feel will most assist you in researching the matters you mentioned, notably whether dragons can talk and how to wake one. My intuition tells me that you might be considering the White Lady in this regard, in which respect I draw your attention to the story of the Icebound Spear. I knew of the fabled item's existence, but it did not occur to me that it might have been in the repository. If I had realised, I would never have allowed Maddileh to take it since its purpose is not to kill but to disable.*
>
> *If the spear is the same, no human has ever witnessed its use—not even Tertian—so I cannot say for certain what will happen if you remove it. However, see the pages I highlighted about how dragons take nourishment from words. This could be a way to ensure no lasting damage is done.*
>
> *I remain your faithful servant,*
> *Lady Wren Weldrake*

Tertian? The name was unfamiliar, but she saw that one of the books was entitled *The Tales of Tertian*, so she turned to this first. Her aunt had marked the foreword with one of her signature placeholders—a strip of thick paper with a pressed flower on it. "Just because a thing is functional," Wren used to say, "does not mean it can't have an element of beauty too." Maddileh ran a finger over the bookmark and was filled with an unexpected burst of affection. Her childhood had been made almost unbearable by her parents, but her aunt had always had a smile for her or a quiet place where she could hide from her father's moods and her mother's intolerable demands. Seeing the letter and the bookmark made Maddileh suddenly ashamed that she hadn't gone home and braved her parents' displeasure so that she might see her aunt again. After all, Wren Weldrake knew well what Maddileh suffered because she suffered it also.

Still, one problem at a time.

Focusing on the book, Maddileh read as follows:

Before becoming Troubadour Tertian, I was known as Distinguished Mage Weldrake. I know my father frowned on my taking the name of my aunt when I went into train- ing, but he has my three elder brothers to carry on his name, and I felt that my aunt (and my sister, who will necessarily follow in her footsteps) deserved some recognition beyond the walls of our own fort.

Perhaps it was a foolish affectation, but I wonder now, as I sit in the Dragon Council's chamber, whether there was perhaps the guiding hand of the Allfather in this, for it is said that from his far-reaching chariot in the sky, he can see not only the whole fourteen realms but the future too. Did he see that I was destined to join the Mage Guild only to leave it to fulfil a life as a troubadour—and a renegade one at that? For it is not human tales I collect here but dragon tales.

I can imagine that the first criticism thrown at this

book is that I made up all the stories herein because dragons can't talk. I can disagree with that theory, but I cannot disprove it. Centuries ago, after the Fireborne Blade was forged, there came the Breach—that is the dragon name for it; there is no human term since, according to our records, it never happened. Our older stories say that dragons can talk, but our modern histories (most influential being, of course, The Demise and Demesne of Dragons*) make no mention of it. I can't possibly be the first mage to consider why such a contradiction exists, but it appears I am the first to try to find out* why *it exists.*

According to the dragons, the Breach was when all dragons took an oath to cease talking to humans. Over time, later generations of dragons lost the ability. While the older ones still retain the talent, they can only speak to certain humans—those excepted when the oath was taken (the dragons say "oath," but its far-reaching effect makes me certain magic was involved). Some humans were deemed worthy exceptions (or possibly begged to be—again, dragon history is murky here), and so not all communication between humans and dragons has been lost.

It would seem that my family is one of the exceptions, a fact that does not surprise me given the Weldrake Legacy (see The Well Dragon, *page 95), but it leaves me with an impossible situation: only I and a select few can hear them, so even if I wanted to prove that dragons can talk, I could not.*

Maddileh laid the book on her knees, her thoughts whirling. *Why didn't Aunt Wren show me this before I went dragon hunting? I would have . . .*

What? Given up my chance at redemption based on some dusty old book? To her shame, Maddileh felt sure she would have not.

Well, that changes now.

Maddileh spent the rest of the day reading what her aunt had sent her, making notes that she shared with Saralene later that night. Saralene had bowed out of a dinner with a representative from the First Realm, sending two of the most revered mages in her place. With the windows shut and additional spells around the walls to prevent eavesdropping, Saralene and Maddileh sat before the fire with the books spread around them and a light supper of broth, barley bread, and onion tarts nearby while Maddileh explained what she'd discovered.

"Have you ever heard of the Icebound Spear before?" Saralene asked.

"No, but not even Aunt Wren was sure it existed. It wasn't forged by or for humans, you see. It was completely dragon-made and was designed to punish and incapacitate dragons who had committed a crime of some sort."

"Made with the horn of a northern unicorn," Saralene observed, squinting at the passage before her. "If the spear you used is indeed the same spear, then that counts as proof that the snow unicorns exist. It seems the legends are just springing to life today." She bit into an onion tart, chewed thoughtfully, then said, "So, assuming the spear you used is this Icebound Spear, then removing it will wake the dragon."

"Yes, although talking to it—sorry, *her*—as well will help. Dragons gain nourishment from words, apparently."

"Then why do they steal sheep and cows from the villages?" Saralene speculated.

"I don't know. The book talks about later dragons having lost the ability to talk, so maybe they became more reliant on food like animals. After all, some dragons have the characteristics of birds or snakes or eels. Who knows how else they changed?"

"Indeed. But you think that if the White Lady can talk, then it's likely she survives on magic and words like the old dragons."

Maddileh shrugged. "It's likely. She is the oldest living dragon we know of."

And whose fault is that? asked a sly voice at the back of her mind.

Saralene's eyes were bright. "Well, it seems we'll be waking a dragon, then."

SEVEN

THE COMING OF SMITH
The Tales of Tertian

In the time before the Breach, gem-stealers* and sky-riders had an uneasy peace.

In general, the two races avoided one another, but then one day, a man and his daughter approached the dragon elders. The dragons were curious because the man smelt of hot metal and soot; they thought, perhaps, he had something to do with the soot drakes that live in their homes.

"I come seeking help," the man declared, "with my life and skills in payment."

"And what is your skill?" asked Megrana. "For your life is of little interest to us."

"I am a smith." The sky-riders knew not what this was, so he explained, "You have many tons of earth-ribbons in your home. I could fashion you whatever you wished: drinking bowls for fresh spring water, great rings for your talons, crowns for your head, mirrors to reflect your magnificence."

---

* The gem-stealers earned their name by pilfering treasure from the gold-guards. It is unclear whether the sky-riders also contributed to the situation by stealing treasure from the humans too, but the legend-tellers are (unsurprisingly) silent on this point (and when a dragon is telling you a story, you don't interrupt them with impertinent questions).

"And what skill has the small gem-thief?" another dragon asked.

The girl stepped forward and curtsied. "Great dragon, I have not the skills of my father, though perhaps I could learn them in time. But my body is smaller than yours. I can be a gem-finder for you, not a thief. The coins and jewels that have fallen into crevasses my nimble fingers can retrieve. The corners that remain clogged with dirt I can sweep. The silver that is tarnished I can polish."

The Dragon Council dismissed the humans while they discussed the matter. Upon calling them back, Mienylyth spoke thus: "We care not for crowns—they are an egg-cracker invention for oppressors. But the other items we like, and we can think of many more. Our breath is too hot and our claws too large for the work you describe. Little egg-cracker—while we do not see much value in your work, we deep-dwellers know the value of family, so we will accept your service so you may not be parted from your father."

The girl sank to her knees, tears falling freely. "Oh, thank you, great dragon. Truly, the stories about your cruelty are wrong."

"But first we must hear the other part of the bargain," Mienylyth continued. "What do you seek from us? We sense it is revenge, for your grief hangs about you like an old skin, not yet shed."

"You are correct. My request is for vengeance," said the smith. "I used to have a wife and two daughters. We lived in the human town you see not far distant. My forge was at the edge of town, downwind from the other dwellings so that the smoke and sparks would not blow into town. Many forges in my realm are built this way, but the townsfolk here saw it as a peculiarity. They felt I set up my business at a distance because I thought them unclean. In retaliation, they began to think me unclean. They did not like the customs I brought with me from my old home.

"At every opportunity, my family was spurned. Even those who showed us kindness did so with a superior smile, acting for their own sakes rather than ours. I wished to move away, but I had sunk much money into my forge, and to depart would have left us impoverished. Furthermore, while the townsfolk disliked us, they still brought us business. They might grumble about my prices, but they never grumbled about my work.

"I do not know if you are aware, great dragon, but raiders from the Second Realm have been troubling this land. They descended on our homes three nights past. They were drawn to my forge in particular for its store of weapons. I have good strong doors and heavy shutters, but one of them dropped a bag of powder down the chimney onto the forge fire. In moments, the room was filled with a vile yellow smoke that filled us with fear and robbed us of air. Perhaps we would have done better to die in there, but the instinct to live is strong, and when we opened the door to run out, the raiders rushed in.

"The smoke made my head spin so my knowledge of what happened next is not clear. But I know that for a night and a day, they tortured my family. I know that the townsfolk huddled in their houses and did not help, even though they could hear our screams."

"Perhaps they feared for their own skins," Megrana suggested. No sky-rider would ignore the screams of a brother or sister, but they knew humans did.

At this point, the girl stood up. "I might have thought so

too, great dragon, if I had not been sheltering with some. I had been delivering nails to a carpenter when the raid struck. Initially, he and his wife hid me inside with them, but when they realised that the raiders were torturing my family, they took it into their heads that my presence would bring them danger, so they cast me out.

"I ran from house to house, pleading through doorways and windows for help. No one let me in, although one man did open the door and try to encourage me closer, but when I saw the rope in his hands, I knew he meant to tie me up and leave me for the raiders. Indeed, when I ran away, he opened the door and called out, 'She's going that way!'" The ground beneath both father and daughter was sodden with tears.

"When the raiders finally left, I snuck back into the forge and found only my father alive. With the raiders gone, I thought some townsfolk would now help me, but although some doors opened to my urgent knocking, it was only so those inside could throw things at me until I went away.

"I gathered what supplies I could and helped my father into the woods, where I healed him as best I could. Then we came to you."

The dragons collected the tears of both humans on their tongues, for tears contain the echoes of emotions and memories, and the dragons tasted their truth.

"This is a ghastly* tale you bring us," Mienylyth said, "and we ache for your suffering. What would you have us do?"

Smith and his daughter exchanged a glance before he said, "I had hoped to ask you to kill the raiders and the

---

* Ghosts and ghasts are, in fact, terrible tormentors to dragons, so "a ghastly tale" is the worst kind for a dragon.

townsfolk too—the one for killing my family, the other for hiding when they should have helped and for offering up my daughter to save their skins. But my daughter spoke to me lengthily in the woods, and while I hate the townsfolk with all the bile in my guts, I will abide by her kind heart and ask only that you raze the town to the ground. I will request only that they lose their homes as I have lost mine."

An approving rumble ran through the dragons. "We appreciate your wisdom, dirt-walker. You come to us drenched with blood, and if you had demanded the blood of innocents, even cowardly innocents, we would not have deemed it a good bargain. But we will turn these raiders into raven-harvest and destroy the dwellings of the other egg-crackers. This bargain is acceptable to us."

The dragons proceeded to do just that, while Smith and his daughter were given a special potion to drink. It boiled their insides and gave them a day of agony, but the dragons promised they would survive many, many years if they drank the potion once every year. Which they did.

Smith's enduring legacy included the Fireborne Blade, the Icebound Spear, the Resurrection Dish, and the Earth Axe, among many others.

HOW THE DRAGONS GOT A BLACKSMITH
Troubadour Tales

There was once a skilled smith who was the best in all the fourteen realms. People would come from far and wide for his wares. Even kings would humbly seek out his services and ask, with great humility, if he might attend to their mighty swords.

The dragons, who lived nearby, heard of his talents, and their minds began to ponder. "Think of the beautiful things he could make for us," they whispered to one another. "Crowns, rings, swords, bejeweled mirrors. We must have him for our own."

So, one night, a brace of these sly creatures swept down from their mountain and stole the smith away. To ensure he stayed with them, they also took his daughter, whom they kept in a big cage; they only let her out to clean their filthy caves. "We will eat her if you don't do as we say," they threatened.

To make sure he could never go back to his old life, they razed the town to the ground and killed everyone there. Some were burned, and some were carried high up into the air and dropped, screaming, to their deaths.

Yet out of such tragedy bloomed hope, for it was the dragons' blacksmith who forged the Fireborne Blade that would one day save all fourteen realms.

EIGHT

That night, Saralene found herself in the Gravelands again. Luciel was setting out rose petals to dry in the hot, still air. She looked up at Saralene, who felt sick and heavy, as if full of flu. "You'd best hurry back," Luciel said. "He's getting better at this, and he'll be able to close the channel soon."

She was speaking the truth: although Saralene could hear Maddileh calling her name, it was faint and distorted.

"Not that I wouldn't prefer your company to his," Luciel added as Saralene struggled to her feet. With a sigh, she looked down at the petals before her. "Perhaps you could tell me what is wrong with my roses."

Saralene managed to find the thread of Maddileh's voice and focused on her room at the palace, which was barely visible. This time, as Hosh flew in the opposite direction, he was laughing. Saralene arrived back in her body trembling with frustration and fear. "We need to stop this, and soon," she whispered into Maddileh's ear as the two women knelt on the bed, embracing tightly. Saralene should have felt aglow at having Maddileh's arms around her, but all she felt was numb and terrified.

"Tomorrow," Maddileh whispered softly. "We'll go tomorrow."

———

Maddileh would have preferred to have ridden to the White Lady's demesne, but the journey would take them close to two weeks, and from the waxen pallor of Saralene's face, she didn't think they had that long. That meant traveling by magic was the only option, however undesirable, and so Maddileh stood in the circle, as bid, and waited for Saralene to complete the preparations.

When all was ready, Saralene stepped into the circle and took Maddileh's hands. "This will be sudden and unpleasant."

Saralene was right on both counts. One moment, they were standing in the palace gardens; the next, the world shifted as if invisible hooks inside Maddileh had tugged her sideways, obliging her skin to follow where her guts were already going. For a few awful moments, she felt no ground beneath her feet, and all the air was sucked out of her lungs. And then the internal tugging stopped with a suddenness that made it feel like she'd been punched. The two of them sank to their knees, gasping and retching for a few moments until they felt strong enough to get up.

Maddileh's relief at the ordeal being over was swiftly subsumed by dread at finding herself outside the White Lady's lair. Again. This place held nothing but unpleasant memories for her.

Allfather's balls, what's the matter with you? A mage party came and went without incident. And you have to go inside, dangerous or not. She forced herself to straighten and walked over to Saralene, who was gazing up at the lair entrance.

"It's so big. As tall as the halls in the palace," Saralene murmured.

"The inside is even more impressive," Maddileh replied,

already heading for the entrance. If she kept her momentum going, it would be fine; if she stopped long enough for her thoughts to catch up, she'd be in trouble.

Maddileh walked the tunnel with a constant prickle at the back of her neck. If the White Lady was only asleep, did that mean the dragon-dead were still here? Was Petros lurking in the shadows, ready to seize her body and kick out her soul? She repressed a shudder.

When they finally reached the cavern, Maddileh saw that both her dreams and her memories were correct, if chronologically incompatible. Now that she looked closely, she could detect hints of old carvings in the pillars long worn away; if she hadn't known to look for them, she wouldn't ever have spotted them.

The White Lady was just as she was in the dream, although more awe-inspiring when viewed with real eyes. They approached carefully, Maddileh half expecting the dragon to open one golden eye before engulfing them in flames. But the White Lady slept on, her scales glittering with frost, the spear jutting out of her gums.

Stepping forward, Maddileh gripped the spear and asked, "Ready?"

"Ready," Saralene agreed, wrapping her hands lower down the shaft. On the count of three, they pulled the spear free from the dragon's flesh; Maddileh had thought they'd need all their strength, but it slid out easily. Taking an oil-cloth from her bag, Saralene wiped the dragon's blood from the tip, folded the cloth so the bloodstain was on the inside, and put the cloth away. "Just in case it comes in useful," she said in response to Maddileh's questioning look.

With the tip now clean, Maddileh examined it and saw

that what she'd taken to be some kind of enchanted metal or stone did, in fact, look as if it was made of horn. Examining the shaft, she recognised pictograms carved on the metal bands, just like the pillars of the cavern.

"The wound is almost closed," Saralene said, pointing. Maddileh couldn't help feeling a little relieved. She'd worried that dragon blood would gush forth, bringing in its slippery wake some awful death. "Shall we tell stories, then, to feed her up?" It was a ridiculous thing to say but—

Yes. The voice was louder, and while it was still inside Maddileh's head, it also seemed to echo around the cave. Saralene jumped and looked around, wild-eyed.

"You heard it too?" Maddileh asked. Saralene nodded, and Maddileh felt strangely comforted; she wasn't alone, or mad.

Keeping a careful watch on the dragon, the two of them set up a little camp near the White Lady's head. When settled, Maddileh took out Tertian's book. It had occurred to them that most of the stories Maddileh knew were of heroic knights—hardly the best stories to tell a sick dragon. So they'd determined to read Tertian to her, and they passed the book between them, taking it in turns to read. As they did so, the frost on her skin began to recede, but by the time they'd finished the book, the frost was only a third of the way gone.

Maddileh and Saralene looked at each other, Maddileh desperately trying to think of stories she could tell that might not piss off a slumbering dragon when Saralene declared, "The Bloodless Princes," and began to recount the tale of the rulers of Findara. Then Maddileh offered up the story of the Waiting Woman. Between them, they managed to remember enough folk and fairy tales to take the frost three-quarters of the way across the dragon's body. The thaw was spreading out from the wound so that all that now remained frozen was the back end and tail of the dragon, yet still the White Lady lay immobile, her eyes open but unfocused.

"I don't know any more folktales," Maddileh whispered. "Do you think we can read Tertian again?"

"It might be unwise," Saralene said. She thought for a moment, then said, "When I was ten, my brother cut all my hair off." Maddileh stared at her. "It was the first time he had ever been in trouble over me. I was supposed to forgive his pinches and pushes as boyish behaviour. If there was punishment for a broken cup or a dent in a door, mine would be double his because I was older and should know better. I wept silently as the cane fell on my hands and legs, then I walked away as calmly as I could. On the rare occasions he was caned, Petros would weep and wail, and my mother would gather him into a hug after and wipe away his tears, saying the balance was restored. The punishment had equaled and therefore canceled out the crime.

"But when he cut my hair, both my parents were furious. It was my father who whipped him—a sign of seriousness since children's discipline in our house was always the women's remit. When he was well and truly whipped, my brother turned in tears to our mother, hoping to be soothed. But Mother stood stony-faced and said, 'The punishment cannot fit the crime because it will take months for her hair to grow back, and all that time, your father and I will see that misdemeanour before us, fresh and offensive.'

"She sent him to his room, and they were both hard on him for a good week—until, of course, he wormed his way back into their graces by . . . well, by being a boy. Later, I found out that the reason they were so angry was not because of the hurt he'd caused me by cutting great lumps of my hair off but because a daughter with her head all ragged would be a disgrace to them. But I still get a warm glow when I think of his snotty red face, so disbelieving at the unfairness of it all." Saralene grinned, and Maddileh found herself grinning back. "Your turn. Tell me something from your childhood."

Maddileh thought for a moment, then said, "The day I first picked up a sword, then. That one still sticks in my memory."

For the next few hours, they passed stories back and forth, learning more about each other with every tale. If Maddileh had been uncertain before about whether she loved Saralene, all doubt vanished when she learned of the trials she'd faced growing up. Only when her stomach growled was the spell broken and their purpose brought back into her mind.

All trace of frost was gone, and the White Lady's eyes were fixed on them. Both women scrambled to their feet, backing away. The White Lady lifted her neck and extended her tail in a stretch. Maddileh felt a thrill of fear as well as awe run through her. Years of training made her hand reach for the blade at her side.

"Welcome, little egg-crackers. I would have greeted you, before but I was . . . indisposed." The dragon focused on Maddileh. "I see that you have the Fireborne Blade now. Did you put it to use?"

Maddileh's hand tightened around the hilt. "Yes."

"And who did you kill with it?"

Maddileh shifted uncomfortably. "No one."

The dragon had no eyebrows, but the ridged scales above her eyes lifted. "You retrieved this legendary man-fang, and you did not use it?"

"Having it was enough," Maddileh said. "Everyone knows the legend. Retrieving it was sufficient to prove my worth."

"Is that so? How extraordinary. And you say everyone knows the legend. I have heard the man-songs that you gem-stealers tell of this blade, and they do not match our own tales." She glanced at *The Tales of Tertian*. "A fact that might not surprise you if you have read that."

"Who told you our tales?" Saralene asked. "Was it Tertian?"

The dragon's head swiveled so she could focus entirely on Saralene. "Certainly, the tale-carrier told us some, but I have listened to your kind for many years and learned much."

"You listened? When?"

"Curled up outside doorways. On a vantage point above your celebrations. If you have spoken to Lady Weldrake, you will know that we dragons live on words. We consume them the way you consume heavy-beasts and ground-clouds."

"You mean cows and sheep, I think," Saralene said. "Those descriptions were in Tertian's tales."

The dragon lowered her head and peered intently at Saralene. "You are a puzzle. You have not the ancient lineage of this other dirt-walker that allows her to hear me, but there is something in your blood that responds to my voice. You smell of dragon." Her nostrils flared. "Ah! And of serpent-stone. You have both used the Resurrection Bowl. Together, yes? So your blood mingled.

"But you," she said to Saralene, "did not come through the process intact. I see a thread tying you to your underworld. Tell me what happened."

Haltingly, Saralene recounted the story. The dragon remained eerily still during the retelling; not once did the creature blink. When Saralene was finished, there was a deep rumbling in the White Lady's chest, and Maddileh's fingers instinctively went to the sword again. The dragon's eyes narrowed. "It means I'm thinking, egg-cracker, not that I'm about to eat you."

"I have a name, you know," Maddileh said coldly.

"So do I."

"Yes, the—" Maddileh stopped. Dragons had their own tales and their own language. Why shouldn't they have their own names? She was thinking of them as beasts again. With great effort, she let go of her sword and inclined her head. "My apologies. What is your name?"

The dragon's gums pulled back, revealing her sharp teeth; a wave of terror surged through Maddileh until she realised the dragon was smiling. "That was well done, dirt—human. My name is Mienylyth."

"Maddileh."

"Saralene."

There was a moment of stillness between the three of them, and Maddileh sensed that something had shifted.

Turning to Saralene, Mienylyth said, "Your resurrection was powerful and well crafted. No trace of it remains except for the smell of dragon, which accompanies all workings of the Resurrection Bowl. Maddileh's form is solid and centred, no chinks through which the previous soul might climb into the body." Maddileh felt a knot inside her un-knit; until that moment, she hadn't realised how much she'd silently worried that Petros might do as Hosh had done. "I believe the weakness in your own working was introduced by the man you replaced. I warrant he laid down measures against being killed during his life span. If you keep finding yourself in Luciel's garden, then there must be something hidden there that tethers him. When you return, look for something out of place and then focus your mind on it. You should be able to sense the magic, since an enchantment to keep him there would have to be strong."

"And if I find this hidden thing, it will prevent him from taking over my body again?"

For the first time since she'd woken, Mienylyth looked away from the humans. "It will not. Your flesh is the link, and the only way to be rid of him is to be rid of your flesh."

"But then, wouldn't I be really . . . dead?"

"Yes. But it is the only way. He is playing a game, so you must sweep his pieces away and set up a new board."

"That is your solution," Saralene said, her voice flat. "I must die and let him have this body."

"No. He will not have your body. When he next takes over it, I shall burn the flesh from his bones. He will descend to the Gravelands, untethered. You will already be in Luciel's garden. You will be without your flesh, but you will not be dead. I know a way into your underworld. If your Champion has the courage"—her gaze flicked to Maddileh—"then she and I can enter and beseech the lords of your underworld to return you to the lands of the living. The Fireborne Blade, in the hands of Death, can cut through worlds. It is not a certain solution, but it is a solution."

"Why would you help us?" Maddileh asked, suspicion souring her words.

"One life for many lives," Mienylyth said simply. "I help you and, in return, you let me and all other sky-riders live in peace. Unharmed. Unhunted. That is the bargain I offer you."

"We could do it," Saralene said as they stood a little distance away. "It's in my power as High Mage to make such a rule."

"No. It's in your power to advise the emperor that such a rule should be made. You cannot enforce it. And if we cannot promise our end of the bargain, then we're going to find ourselves with an incredibly unhappy dragon who feels she's been cheated."

"But think of the alternative. Not my life—if I have to give it up in service to the fourteen realms, I will. But we can't let Hosh back into this body. His machinations and greed were dragging the realms backward. Think of all I've achieved in these last few years," Saralene pleaded. "I can't let that go to waste. Even if we can't keep the bargain with Mienylyth, we should at least let her kill me so—"

"No! I won't let that happen. How would we get you back anyway? She talks about beseeching the Bloodless Princes to let you return, but what if they don't? Speedwell and Otanna and the rest are just stories. We can't know how likely it is they'll let you go. Or me, for that matter, if I turn up with a bloody big dragon in tow."

"Agreed, but really, Maddileh, what are our other options? I see none."

This conversation went round and round Maddileh's head as she tramped around the cave. She and Saralene had been sent in opposite directions to search for the necklace Petros had given his sister. "It is a serpentstone," Mienylyth had explained, "the brain of a sister sky-rider. Just as the Resurrection Bowl will raise you from death, so this will help you in the underworld." Frustratingly, she had refused to say how it might help, only that it was a last resort. Such secrecy and other vagueness in the plan made Maddileh incredibly uneasy.

But again she kept circling back to Saralene's answer: What other options were there?

Just as her eye was caught by the glitter of what she sought, a scream echoed through the cavern.

"Gem-stealer! Quick! He comes!"

Maddileh snatched up the necklace and raced back to where she'd left Saralene and Mienylyth to find her friend crumpled on the floor, her face contorted in agony. Her skin was rippling in a sickening manner as if something moved through her flesh.

"The serpentstone—quickly! Put it in her hands. She must have it when she traverses the channel."

Maddileh raced forward, prised open Saralene's fingers, and wrapped them around the necklace. Then, to her shame, she backed swiftly away; the feel of that shifting skin beneath her hands had been revolting.

"Why is he coming now? He normally comes at night," she said, having to shout to be heard over Saralene's screams. Each one pierced her brain like a knife.

"He can sense my magic. It will draw him like crows to carrion."

Saralene was panting, her eyes unseeing, and she clutched the stone to her chest a moment before her body convulsed. Then suddenly, it was not her beautiful face there but the jubilant one of Hosh, his eyes blinking blearily, his hands empty.

The old man got unsteadily to his feet, cackling at his own cleverness. When he looked up and saw Mienylyth towering above him, his eyes widened in shock and awe. "A dragon," he breathed before making an awkward bow. "Greetings, most noble creature."

Mienylyth inclined her head solemnly and replied, "Greetings." And Maddileh was suddenly certain that the dragon had tricked them.

"I wonder if I might—" began Hosh, and then fire was spewing out of Mienylyth's mouth and billowing around him. He briefly became a bright white figure of burning lines before being lost in the fury of the blaze. When Mienylyth closed her mouth, all that remained was a pile of ash on the floor—ash in which the knight sensed movement.

Maddileh moved closer and saw leechlike creatures writhing in the mess. One or two of them opened mouths lined with needle-teeth to emit piercing shrieks.

"I have done all I can," Mienylyth said. "Now it is your turn. You must kill what remains."

Unsheathing her sword, Maddileh stabbed the tip into each loathsome creature in turn. Some exploded, guts going from inside to out; others shriveled and writhed, acrid black smoke pouring off their skin. All of them screamed.

When they were all finally dispatched, Mienylyth said solemnly, "Now you have slain something with the Fireborne Blade. It is truly yours."

Maddileh looked at the sword in her hand, then cast it to the floor before walking away to find a quiet corner.

I didn't get to say goodbye, she thought. She felt the urge to cry, but the tears would not come, and all she could do was curl up and shake uncontrollably.

NINE

THE BLOODLESS PRINCES
Troubadour Tales

At the beginning of the world, those who died went to the Gravelands, where they wandered. As more and more souls died, the Gravelands became a miserable place. While the dead were free from bodies that could be affected by pain and suffering, and liberated from souls shackled to woe, they were not free from the machinations of others. Soon there was bloodshed and fighting. While the dead could feel no pain from the living world, their souls were not immune to injuries inflicted in the Gravelands themselves.

Busy with the blossoming world above, the gods were unaware of the travails in the Gravelands until ten maidens made an effort to escape and bring news of the terrible events unfolding. Only one maiden reached the Allmother to impart the tale, and she was so exhausted that once her tale was told, she sank twice-dead to the ground. The death of the soul leaves nothing behind, but the Allmother did not want the woman's sacrifice to be forgotten, so she took the blue from the woman's eyes and turned it into forget-me-nots, which is why they can often be found growing wild on graves.

The Allmother took such dire news to the Allfather, and

together, they discussed what should be done. The Allfather rode out over the land, proclaiming that there would be a contest to appoint a ruler of the Gravelands. All those who wished to enter had to present themselves at the Plane of Blue Grass by Midsummer's Eve for the contest to begin the following day.

Among the contestants were two princes, C'sava and Pravhan. Despite being identical twins, one of them was the rightful son of the king of the Thirteenth Realm while the other was the son of a mage, the queen's lover. The queen had lain with the mage unaware she was already pregnant, and through some quirk of magic, the mage's seed had taken root as well. In a panic, the mage cast a spell so that even the queen did not know which child was which when they were born, and the king was obliged to adopt both as his heirs in fear of casting aside his own true son.

The brothers had decided that they would both try out for ruler of the underworld, and the unsuccessful brother would be free to return home and take over the living kingdom when their father died. It never occurred to them that someone else might win; for all their differences, both brothers shared a complete conviction of his own superior value—a conviction that, it turned out, was entirely accurate.

Pravhan was a quiet, bookish lad who would pore over maps and law journals, valuing justice and obedience. C'sava was more militarily minded, and found worth in finely honed skills and hard-won victories. To him, a man of action was worth more than a man of letters.

Before the trials began, the Allmother looked into the hearts of each contestant before allowing them to enter. She would not permit a man weak of morals or hard of heart to compete, for such a man should not rule over the dead. Given what happened later, it has been fervently debated whether the Allmother was mistaken or deceived when she allowed the brothers to enter.

Both princes excelled. Pravhan impressed the gods with his steady manner and wise judgment, while C'sava impressed them with his military prowess and battle skills, which could help restore order in the war-torn Gravelands.

The princes progressed through the trials until they were the only two left. However, despite having begun the event by clasping hands and wishing each other luck, a seed of jealousy had now blossomed in the heart of one of the brothers. C'sava saw the sage looks the gods shared when watching Pravhan deliver judgments worthy of Luciel herself. He feared that he would lose out on the final test, and it had become supremely important to him to become ruler of the underworld. He had realised that while the losing brother would rule an earthly kingdom during his lifetime, he would become subject to the kingship of his brother for the eternity that followed. That was most unpalatable.

So, the night before the final trial was due to take place, C'sava slipped into Pravhan's tent and slit his throat, being careful to catch all the blood in a sack made from a dragon's stomach. When the stomach-sack was full and Pravhan was white and bloodless, C'sava carefully sealed the sack and buried the husk of his brother in the ground quite some way from the trial camp.

The next morning, C'sava turned up for his trial and waited with an expression of innocence for Pravhan to arrive—which, of course, he didn't. The trial ground was searched. When that proved fruitless, the Allfather took to the skies and scoured the whole world. The Allmother walked the earth itself, looking for any sign of him. But his beating heart was stilled, his blood stored away, and the empty shell of his body lay crumpled in the ground.

C'sava might have gotten away with it, except that while he'd caught all the blood from Pravhan's body in the stomach-sack, a single drop of blood had fallen unnoticed from the tip of his knife. It was that single spot of blood that the Allmother eventually found as she walked back to the camp. From that speck, she discerned the whole truth, and she hurried to the Allfather, where they silently made their plans.

All the contestants were called to the Plane, with C'sava confident he would be crowned winner. The Allfather stood before them and declared: "We had intended to give the Gravelands to both Pravhan and C'sava to rule over jointly. We still intend this, but first, we must redress the balance."

The Allfather made a small gesture, and a line appeared on C'sava's throat. Every last drop of blood leaked from the prince onto the ground. The Allmother, who had found the stomach-sack, emptied the contents next to it, and Pravhan's ghost rose up to stand by the ghost of his brother. "These Bloodless Princes shall rule over the Gravelands together, since the underworld will benefit from both their skills," the Allfather declared. "But to keep the peace, they shall do so at separate times. Pravhan shall be the prince from when the Deathly Sun rises, C'sava from the moment it sets. For his treachery, C'sava shall be placed in charge of the Night City, where all the sinful and unworthy individuals reside. Pravhan, who has been greatly wronged, shall rule over the

Peaceful City, where the good and honest dwell. Say your farewells, brothers, for you shall not meet again."

And so the two Bloodless Princes were installed in the city of Findara, and order came to the Gravelands.

TEN

Saralene scrambled to her feet, the necklace clutched to her chest, and found herself alone in Luciel's garden. Her heart was hammering fast—or was it? She placed a hand on her chest and felt nothing stirring beneath her skin. Yet she was sure she could hear her heartbeat thudding in her ears.

Her gaze was drawn to the Perilous Bridge; Luciel was standing on the near side, waiting, while a figure staggered over from the darkness. Recognising Hosh, Saralene hurried to the garden wall, peering at the distant scene. Luciel started across the bridge, meeting Hosh when he was two-thirds across. At this distance, Saralene couldn't hear voices or discern faces, but she did see Hosh look in her direction and had to resist the childish urge to duck below the wall.

Hosh tried to continue, but Luciel put out a hand to stop him. He pushed her aside, and for an awful moment, Saralene thought the woman might fall into the abyss. But Luciel easily kept her feet and turned to watch Hosh proceed. From the abyss, crawling over the stone bridge, came twisting tendrils of black that moved like smoke but with the weight of flesh. They surged across the bridge behind Hosh, wrapping around him. He screamed as they overwhelmed him and dragged him down into the darkness. That same scream echoed, fading, diminishing, until the abyss claimed him utterly.

Saralene shuddered. She had despised the man, but see-ing someone hauled down into damnation was still pitiable.

When Luciel returned to her garden, she looked at Sara-lene and said, "Interesting. How are you here?"

"It's . . . complicated," Saralene admitted, "and it was a dragon's idea. I'm not sure I followed it all."

And now that I'm here, I'm not sure if Maddileh wasn't right and this will all turn out badly. A wave of grief overcame her then. What if she never saw Maddileh again? Her chest tightened at the thought of never telling her friend how much she loved her. They hadn't even said goodbye.

A softness entered Luciel's eyes. "A dragon. I miss them. They provided great counsel in my day. I hear they don't speak now, so you must have a special gift if you can under-stand them. Now, with the greatest respect, do you think you could get out of my garden?"

"I would very much like to. I need to find the Bloodless Princes and ask one of them to send me back to the world of the living."

Luciel cocked her head. "Really? And what will you offer them in return?"

"Offer . . . ? Well, I don't know. We didn't get as far as planning that. Matters overtook us somewhat. I'm hoping they'll see my worth, like in the stories, and . . ." She trailed off, seeing Luciel's sceptical expression. She thought about the serpentstone around her neck. Perhaps Mienylyth had ensured she did have something to bargain with after all.

"Well, before you can seek out the Princes, you will need to leave this garden, and so we are back to where we started."

"Your garden, yes." Saralene looked around. "Something is hidden here that tethered Hosh. If I can find it, I can leave. Have you noticed anything strange? Out of place?" Luciel frowned.

"No. But let us search—perhaps I overlooked something."

The two of them searched the garden from end to end, checking the walls, among the plants, under stones, and even in the stream that ran alongside the house; there was nothing. Now and again, Saralene would reach out with her mind to search for cunning illusions, but the whole place was crafted from the Allfather's enchantments, so while she could detect the single discordant note of Hosh's working, she could not pinpoint it among the overwhelming amount of pure magic.

The sky above them was filled with clouds in motion. There was no sun evident, despite the mention of the Deathly Sun in the myths; instead, the realm was illuminated by an unseen light source. At one point during the search, the clouds rolled away to reveal a starlit sky, empty of moon. The world became a little gloomier, a moonlit night with no moon.

Saralene sat down on the grass, her legs and back aching from her exertions. "I thought the afterlife had no bodily pains," she said, wincing as she massaged a calf.

"It generally does not, unless one of the Princes wills it otherwise," Luciel said, sitting near her. "To a certain extent, the normal rules do not apply to you, because you came here in a different manner. You did not pass the Perilous Bridge, so I do not know what pains or powers you will have in the Gravelands. But I do know this: The power of bringing life from death is reserved for the gods. If you seek the Princes to intervene, you must reach them before three days have passed or they will not be able to help you. Their power only extends to rejuvenating what life is left in you, and that life will slowly seep away the longer you are here. If there is no life, they can do nothing. As the days progress, you will find yourself growing pale and listless. Your skin will start to slacken, getting ready to moult like a snakeskin. Once your living skin sloughs off you, your life force will be gone, and you will have to remain among the dead."

Saralene shuddered; that was an obstacle she had not anticipated. "Thank you for that warning. Are you able to tell me what the Princes are like?"

Luciel seemed lost in thought for a moment. "They are . . . not as you expect them. There is no true growth here, so they have not grown as people over the centuries. Instead, they have . . . *condensed* I think is the best description. Those traits they possessed when they came here have been amplified. Do not walk into Findara with preconceptions or you might find yourself in one of Pravhan's dungeons."

Saralene frowned. "You mean C'sava's dungeons? Pravhan rules over the Peaceful City and the good souls."

"Pravhan values justice above all, and I have learned that justice is like iron: everyone can forge it into a different type of weapon."

Things were starting to look unnervingly difficult and uncertain. Looking around for a means of distraction, Saralene's gaze fell on the rose petals scattered underneath their bush. As she watched, one rose petal fell gently to the ground, then another from a different flower head. *Look for something out of place,* Mienylyth had said. When Saralene had been here previously, Luciel had talked about there being something wrong with her roses.

Leaning over, Saralene picked up a petal; there was no echo of magic in it. "Have your roses always shed like this?"

"No. Not until . . ." They shared a glance and then moved closer to the rosebush. Saralene ran her hands over the flowers, the leaves, the stems. The hint of sour magic was stronger near the roots.

"I think it might be buried beneath the roses," she said. "Have you a trowel?"

Luciel fetched two, and they started scooping earth out from around the base of the bush. Saralene had no idea what to look for; perhaps an enchanted jewel poisoning the soil? She only saw the wormlike creature wrapped around the plant's root ball because it tightened its dark grey coils while she was looking directly at it. "There!" she cried. The two women dug faster, exposing more roots until they could tug the plant upwards. Its roots pulled out of the soil, but the worm's tail was anchored in the earth. They tried jabbing at it with the trowels, but its skin was as hard as metal.

"Wait here," Luciel said before hurrying inside the house. She returned with a rolling pin. "Pull up the bush a little more." Saralene did so, and Luciel tugged hard, pulling more of the worm out of the ground and wrapping it tightly around the rolling pin. Then she started to twist the pin in her hands, wrapping the worm's body around it like a winch, pulling it out of the ground. The worm fought back, almost managing to slide off the end, but Saralene dropped the bush and lent her aid. Soon, the pin was almost covered by the slick grey coils.

"Allmother save us—just how much is there?" Saralene exclaimed as they winched up more and more of the struggling creature. When the pin was covered almost three times over and Saralene's arms were aching, the head of the creature suddenly pulled free. It had a tiny, hairless human face. The release was so sudden the women almost dropped the rolling pin, but in an instant, Saralene gripped the creature just below its loathsome head and muttered a disintegration spell. The worm writhed and bucked in her hands, then abruptly went still. Saralene didn't stop chanting until the melted body slipped through her fingers like glue.

"That's quite disgusting," Luciel said, pulling a face at the slime coating her rolling pin. "You don't know a cleaning spell, do you?"

Saralene took the rolling pin from her. "I think it's a testament to the fact that most mages have been male that no one has thought to create a halfway decent cleaning spell. Soap and water is the best magic I can offer you."

Getting to her feet, Luciel said, "Then I shall fetch those for you, replant the roses, and make us some supper."

"No need for replanting," Saralene said, pointing. The rosebush was hauling itself across the soil by its roots; it slid into the hole, then used its roots to cover itself with soil once more.

After scraping most of the ichor off with a knife, Saralene scrubbed the rolling pin ferociously, reflecting on the fact that of all her ideas of how she might spend her time in the underworld, washing up had not featured. By the time she was done, tantalising smells were coming from the house. Hunger surprised her. Did she have to eat or just want to? After all, soul cakes were routinely offered at funerals to the deceased, so perhaps the dead did eat.

But why is my stomach working and my heart not? she wondered as she cleaned dead worm from her hands. She was breathing too, which seemed natural but not necessary; when she experimentally stopped, it didn't result in the panicked pressure of desperate lungs. She glanced towards the city. *Is this how all the dead are?* She'd know soon enough.

The interior of Luciel's home was sparsely furnished, but what adornments it boasted were clearly valuable, such as the soft rugs on the floor and the grand clock in the entrance hall. In the dining room, Luciel had laid out a meal of smoked haddock flan, potato pancakes, vegetable stew, mustard-glazed carrots and turnips, and a mushroom pâté with crisp flatbreads.

"Where do you get everything?" Saralene asked as she loaded her plate.

"I grow most of it—that's why there's no meat here. The Allfather did provide me with rabbits to stew and sheep to make into mutton, but I much prefer to see them roaming free. It's company, of a sort."

"But you have fish," Saralene said, taking a bite of the flan; it was rich and salty.

"Some swim down the stream now and again."

When they had finished, Luciel put the remains into a bag. "This should see you to Findara, where they have their own food. This mushroom pâté is fine to eat because I grow them in my garden. But don't eat any mushrooms offered to you in Findara."

"Why not?"

"Best not to ask or know. When you get there, do not announce yourself immediately. Be circumspect. Watch. Look. Listen to the whispers in the houses and taverns at night. You may find neither the Night City nor the Peaceful City quite as you anticipate. I shall send your friends after you when they come."

Surprised, Saralene asked, "You know about them?"

Luciel gave her a weary smile. "I know lots of things. Good luck, and stay safe."

ELEVEN

Given that people died all the time, Saralene had expected to meet some on her journey to Findara, but she had the road to herself. Now and again, she caught sight of a sheep wandering around or glimpsed a rabbit in the long grass.

Findara had a high wall around it and large sturdy gates that were open when she reached them. They looked defensive, but with the endless empty fields stretching out under a sky full of clouds, Saralene wondered what threat they might be guarding against. She'd been careful to walk through the night and time her arrival during the day so that she entered the Peaceful City rather than the Night City. The buildings inside were functional but elegant; there was no thatch in sight, only slick roof tiles. The streets were thronged with people, noisy but not overwhelming, and as she walked through the crowds, Saralene felt that she might have been in any living city where daily life carried on. Women hefted washing baskets on their hips; stallholders shouted their wares (all fresh, nothing spoiled); children ran here and there, dodging cuffs from those they nearly tripped up. At one point, Saralene had to step aside while a troupe of dancers in bright clothes twirled and clapped their way down the street, a small group of musicians following them. From inside a theatre came cheers and riotous laughter. It seemed the afterlife was bustling.

The only thing missing from the city was animal life. A normal street would have pigeons and sparrows fluttering through the high places, cats slinking between market stalls, dogs trotting alert at their masters' sides. The absence of them, once noted, was continually felt, like a missing tooth. While Saralene knew that the Gravelands had been created by the gods for humans, it saddened her greatly to think she'd never see her birds—or any animals—in her own afterlife.

After walking the streets for several hours, Saralene had no bearings at all. From the road, the city had appeared fairly small and self-contained. But once inside, it seemed vast, and she was struggling to navigate with any firm sense of direction. At the far side of the city, towering above everything else, was a castle—presumably the home of Prince Pravhan. But even though Saralene tried now and then to head directly towards it, she never got any closer. *How am I going to beseech Pravhan to give me life again if I can't even reach him?*

Feeling hungry, Saralene slipped into a side street and nibbled on some of Luciel's food. As she was packing away her rations, the same troupe of dancers came up the main street; Saralene smiled to see them. Truly, the Peaceful City seemed a happy and beautiful place.

But as they passed close to her, small details caught her eye. Only some of the dancers were smiling; others wore grimaces, some looked vacant. Their bare feet were bleeding, but the scarlet footprints instantly soaked into the stone, leaving no trace.

A prickle of unease ran through Saralene, and when the dancers had gone, she looked around the city with new eyes, searching the faces of the people. Mostly, she saw only contentment, but there was the odd hint here or there to indicate that life was not as blissful as perhaps it seemed. Some people looked incredibly tired, and when they stopped to rest, others would help them to their feet with the demeanour of a parent chivvying along a naughty child. Was rest not permitted in the afterlife? When she heard one mother slap her rambunctious child and threaten to send him to the Street of the Crescent Moon, Saralene sought the place out (but only after several enquiries—mentioning the name drew blank stares or frightened glances for the most part). The street was so narrow it would be better called an alley. Down one wall ran two lengths of wood, one on top of the other. There were small holes bored into the lower plank and hinges were set at intervals along the upper plank, so it could be lifted. At various points along the wall stood people with their fingers locked between the two pieces of wood.

Finger pillories, Saralene thought, alarmed. She'd read of such things in ecclesiastical books; some of the more zealous priests had installed them as punishment for those who misbehaved during services. *But why are they in the Peaceful City? Surely this is something for the Night City?*

A little way down the narrow street sat a woman, her child standing on her knees with her little fingers in the pillory. Other children were there too, some standing on boxes while others had to stretch uncomfortably upwards. Appalled, Saralene started forward, but the mother scowled and gestured none too politely for her to go away. Clearly, interference would do more harm than good, and so Saralene left, her mind full of conflicting thoughts.

———

As the light began to change and the overhead clouds peeled back, people started leaving the streets. Saralene knew that Findara was the location for both the Peaceful City and the Night City, but she had no idea how one became the other. However, from the way people were barring doors and closing shutters, being inside seemed crucial to safety. The Night City held no appeal to her; the treacherous C'sava would be unlikely to be merciful.

As well as the necklace and her clothes, Saralene's little mage bag had been transported to the Gravelands with her. In it, she kept ingredients needed for simple communication, seeking, and illusion spells, in case she ever found herself in unexpected danger. Reaching into the pouch now, she brought out the items needed for a seeking spell. She was vague when casting the enchantment, saying only, "Seek out what I need," filling her mind with a single thought: safety. On the ground before her materialised a little white cat; it was scrawny and see-through, but it moved forward with purpose, and she followed. As they made their way through the streets, she was surprised at how many glances the cat got; Saralene was struck again by the melancholia of an afterlife that contained only humans. A small boy called out, "Here, puss!" but the cat ignored him, and his mother hauled him away.

Saralene began to worry that she'd begun this spell too late as the streets got more and more deserted and still the cat showed no signs of stopping. When they turned onto a street that was empty except for an unoccupied wooden chair, Saralene was minded to cancel the spell and knock on doors instead. But the cat jumped up on the chair and looked at a nearby door expectantly. Seconds later, it opened, and a tall woman with short, slightly curled hair came out. "Gracious!" she exclaimed upon seeing the cat. It disappeared, and she stepped back, momentarily startled, before scooping up the chair. Upon seeing Saralene, she said sharply, "Don't dawdle, woman, or you'll be caught by the night. Inside—quick."

Above the door was an inn sign, and Saralene had time to make out the name THE DRAGON'S EYE before she was inside and the door was bolted behind her. A wave of homesickness washed over her: the smell of pies and the tang of old ale; the heat of a roaring fire; the crunch of rushes beneath her shoes. Saralene might have been prohibited from such places when she lived on the Silverlock estate, but during her time as Kennion's apprentice, she'd frequented taverns now and again, and the smell of them always conjured up one unalterable feeling: freedom.

Behind her, the woman said, "New, are you, duck? I'm Penn. Take a seat and I'll bring you something to eat."

"Why is everyone—" Saralene began, but the woman was already gone. She sat down in a corner away from the main body of the crowd but still close enough to feel the warmth of the fire. A slice of vegetable tart with a crunchy breadcrumb topping and a cup of beetroot beer were placed before her by a harassed-looking serving girl, and Saralene devoured the meal eagerly. The beer was warm and clearly past its best, but she didn't care.

As she finished, Penn rejoined her, her cheeks flushed with toil. She'd brought a jug of ale with her; she filled Saralene's cup, poured one of her own, downed it, then poured another. "Allfather's balls but it's busy in here tonight," Penn said. Saralene winced, but Penn grinned. "Gods can't hear you blaspheme down here, duck. We're beyond them now. We're at the mercy of the Princes."

"Mercy? But surely Prince Pravhan is a just and noble—"

"Prince Pravhan is a great prince who loves order and brings peace to us all," Penn said, her voice respectful, her eyes warning.

"So I have heard," Saralene said with equal care.

Penn nodded. "We never lack for food and drink here. No one lives in poverty. There is no fighting in the streets, only dancing." Saralene thought of the bloody footprints. "Trade is good—you only have to think of a thing and it's on a market stall. We live in a truly blessed place, but such order needs discipline to exist."

"Like finger pillories."

"Indeed. People who push, pinch, slap, or steal must have their hands contained until they learn better. The Prince's punishments always fit the crime."

Crime and punishment in the Peaceful City? That can't be right.

"Why do you all gather inside at night?" Saralene asked.

"Outside, the city is now the Night City. If we stay inside with the doors and windows locked, we're safe."

"What's it like in the Night City?"

Penn gave her a thoughtful stare before answering. "Horrible. I think. It's forbidden for a soul to pass from one realm into the other. If Peaceable Folk cross into the Night City, Prince C'sava punishes them. Any Nighters who try to get in here are dealt with by Prince Pravhan. Severely."

"I see," Saralene said, although, in truth, everything seemed murkier than before.

TWELVE

DISSECTING TROUBADOUR TALES

Within bard songs, there are stories of people venturing into the underworld for everything from saving loved ones to proving themselves or retrieving a valuable item. The purpose of some is to show that love conquers all; the moral of others is that you shouldn't try to cheat the inevitable. All of them show an underworld that is fair and just, proving that we have nothing to fear after death.

A selection of stories of love overcoming death follows.

WHY SPEEDWELLS LOVE FORGET-ME-NOTS

A man called Speedwell lost his beloved wife in the cruelest way: she was attacked and eaten by mountain wolves, leaving him not even bones to bury. But still he erected a headstone in the graveyard, which he visited every day, watering the ground with his tears. As his grief drained into the soil, so forget-me-nots grew up. Knowing the story behind them, of how these delicate flowers were in memory of a brave young woman from the Gravelands, Speedwell felt comforted by their presence. In time, he fell in love with the flowers, as if they were still a woman with blue eyes.

Determined not to lose this second love after losing his wife, Speedwell set off in search of her. After traveling all the fourteen realms, he descended into the fifteenth: the Gravelands. There, he questioned everyone he met, but there were more dead souls than hours left in his life, and so eventually, he died down there.

Moved by pity for his search and knowing that he would never find the blue-eyed woman he sought, Prince Pravhan asked the Allmother to intervene. She turned Speedwell into a different blue flower bearing his name, one with petals of darker blue that could grow next to the forget-me-nots he'd cherished.

OTANNA'S PLEA

Otanna was the greatest musician who ever breathed, and when the emperor heard her music, he invited her to live in his palace and play for him every day. Otanna would not leave her beloved family, so the emperor offered them a home as well.

When her sister died at a tragically young age, Otanna traveled to Prince Pravhan's kingdom and begged that she be released to live out the rest of her life. The Prince was of no mind to agree, since death must come to all, but then Otanna played her lyre, performing her most beloved song—one she had written lying in the forest, listening to birdsong.

All in the Gravelands stopped and listened, transported for a moment back to the world of the living. Even Prince Pravhan was not unmoved, but he still would not give in. Rules were rules.

So then Otanna played a new song, one that represented the heartbreak of losing her sister. Everyone covered their ears, unable to bear the awful sadness of it all.

"This," Otanna declared, "is all I can play with sorrow in my heart. If my sister stays dead, I will no longer be able to play as I once did. If she is dead, so is my music."

Distraught at the idea that something so beautiful would be lost forever, Prince Pravhan granted Otanna's request that her sister should live again. The payment for this boon was that they must both live long and happy lives, so that when Otanna died of old age, she would be able to come and play for Pravhan with a heart full of joy. Otanna agreed, and she and her sister returned to the land of the living, where they enjoyed long and happy lives in the court of the emperor.

C'SAVA'S BEST BULL

A farmer had a prize bull that was his best fighter in the bullbaiting ring. It earned him a lot of money and so when it died, he descended into the underworld to ask for it back. Because it had been an irascible creature, he went to Prince C'sava's realm where he was sure it would be.

C'sava was so impressed by the farmer's daring and so amused by the stories he told of the bull's life that he summoned one of his best fighters and turned him into a bull so that the farmer might return with a beast after all.

This bull was even better than the first, and the farmer became even richer than before. However, one day, as he was checking the bull over, it turned and gored him. The instant the farmer's lifeless body hit the floor, the bull itself also fell down dead and returned to his prince's realm.

THIRTEEN

If pressed, Maddileh would have said that the most surprised expressions she'd ever seen had been when she and Saralene took over the bodies of Hosh and Petros. However, that moment was overshadowed when she landed on the balcony of the palace's audience chamber astride a dragon. A council session had been going on inside, and every mage ran screaming out of the room—even, Maddileh was dismayed to notice, the guards. *I thought I taught them better than that.*

Striding in through the open windows, she approached the High Mage's dais. Behind her, Mienylyth followed, able to keep her head at a normal height thanks to the high ceilings. "That's handy," Maddileh observed; she was feeling lightheaded after riding a dragon, something she'd never thought to experience. Mienylyth gave her a look.

"Have you metal-wearers lost all your learning? The ceilings are high because sky-riders often visited to offer counsel to your rulers."

Maddileh stared at her. "But humans and dragons have been enemies since—"

"The Breach, yes. But before that, our two races shared knowledge. Although such stories are left out of your mansongs."

Maddileh looked up at the creature towering over her.

She tried to imagine dragons coming and going at the palace; it was as ludicrous as trying to imagine a purple dog with horns.

"Would you do it again?" Maddileh surprised herself by asking.

"Perhaps. For the right humans."

One of the side doors opened, and Distinguished Mage Kennion stepped through in such a clumsy manner that Maddileh suspected he had been pushed. Looking up at the dragon, his mouth moved silently, and he paled to the colour of milk. With evident effort, he forced himself to look at Maddileh and said, "Champion, you are here alone. Where is the High Mage?"

"You must call a council meeting," Maddileh said. She had no authority to demand such a thing, yet she suspected having a dragon in the room gave her all sorts of new privileges.

"A council meeting? In here?" Kennion's eyes flicked to Mienylyth.

"Yes, Distinguished One. Now."

Watching the mage and guards creep back in was excellent entertainment until Maddileh took pity on them and stationed herself between Mienylyth and them, offering herself as some kind of reassuring barrier. The dragon had curled up in the corner, her white scales taking on the dull grey of the stone behind her. Evidently, she was trying to make herself as unobtrusive as possible, but that could be tricky for a dragon in any enclosed space. Even Maddileh held tension in her spine and shoulder blades, not entirely at ease standing with her back to such a creature.

"The dragon will not hurt you," Maddileh assured the

mages clustered on the other side of the room. The mages exchanged anxious looks; one or two took a hesitant step forward. There was a great rush of air from behind Maddileh, and smoke billowed past her, rolling towards the mages who screamed and raced back out of the room. Turning round, Maddileh glared at Mienylyth. "That was not even a little bit funny," she said severely. Two golden eyes regarded her.

"You speak truth." The dragon's lips pulled back into a toothy smile, ensuring that those brave enough to remain in the room now vacated it swiftly. "It wasn't a little funny, it was very funny."

Eventually, the mages were all reassembled, and Maddileh was able to deliver the version of the truth she thought they would accept: the High Mage had suffered a terrible corruption of the flesh that could only be scoured by dragon fire. Mienylyth had burned the tainted flesh away, and now they were venturing to the Gravelands to recover her. "And we *will* bring her back," Maddileh vowed. "No other High Mage will be appointed in her place. Distinguished Mage Kennion will be regent in her absence."

Burning on the faces of the mages were a thousand questions; some of them were starting to look more curious now than afraid. But questions would have to wait. Maddileh concluded the meeting and sent servants scurrying for supplies while she and Mienylyth headed to the mage repository to get the armour and magical supplies they'd need for the journey. It unnerved Maddileh just how quietly the dragon could move. Even though the beast's head reached the vaulted ceiling, the clack of talons on stone was no louder than the click of dog claws would have been.

However, when it came to the repository, Mienylyth had to squeeze herself inside, not because the ceilings were any lower but because the room was filled with so many items. Yet the dragon moved with grace, knocking nothing over.

"You metal-wearers were always so cunning with your handcrafts," Mienylyth said, examining her distorted reflection in a curved breastplate. Having been so far in awe of this magical, well-spoken creature, Maddileh took pleasure in showing off some of the finest pieces of armour there. She was careful to choose items used in human battles rather than dragon hunts, but she realised too late she'd made a terrible mistake in showing off King Tanton's shield, which sported dragon scales. Her stomach sank to her boots as Mienylyth lowered her head, sniffed, and said coldly, "That was my nephew."

For a long moment, Maddileh looked into those ageless golden eyes. *She's going to kill me. And she'd be right. I'd kill anyone who bragged about slaughtering my family. But at least I'll be with Saralene and—*

The room shook with Mienylyth's laughter; swords rattled in their sheaths, and armour juddered on stands.

"*That* wasn't funny either," Maddileh said, realising that her words were belied by a terrified, manic grin on her face. Mienylyth snorted a small cloud of smoke over her; it smelt like incense.

"When traveling the realms of the dead, it would be wise to take the Resurrection Dish," Mienylyth said, looking around the armoury. "You need food replication potions too and the Fireborne Blade. That is the most important."

"For protection?" Maddileh said, thinking of the ghouls that were said to haunt the Gravelands.

Mienylyth looked at her steadily. "No. For bargaining."

"Bargaining?"

"In my experience, human rulers gift nothing and exchange everything. Stone-eyes for loyalty, titles for soldiers. You didn't think the Princes would release you out of pity, did you?" Maddileh could not meet Mienylyth's gaze. Everything had happened so swiftly she hadn't had much time to think anything at all, but she couldn't deny that such an idea had been in her mind. "A ruler with life to grant will want a hefty price. And the Fireborne Blade is a great prize."

"But . . ." The words *it's mine* were on the tip of her tongue. Maddileh had searched long for that sword. She'd died for it. Twice. It had become part of her. To give it up would be like losing an arm.

"We have many other great things here," she said. "Perhaps the Princes will be tempted by one of those."

Mienylyth shrugged. "You can try, of course. The Resurrection Dish may tempt him. But from its history, I know that the Blade will be of particular interest to at least one of your rulers. Hand it over in return for them using it to send you both home—that sounds like a fair trade."

Mienylyth had a point, but Maddileh was dogged. "In the stories, the Princes are always moved by the undying love one person shows for another." Even to her ears, her voice sounded mulish.

When Mienylyth spoke, it was with sympathy. "While I do not doubt the strength of your heart-feelings, little human, I do doubt the veracity of the tales. Princes are not moved by love. The world would be a different place if they were. Better to go armed with gifts than hopes."

I'll have to take two swords, then, she thought. *I can't risk being unarmed in the land of the dead if I do have to give up the Blade.*

Maddileh toured the repository and the museum, looking for items that might tempt a Prince of Death, reasoning that she could just bring them back if they were unwanted. In the end, she chose two powerful items: the Trinity Ring, which had threefold powers to turn the wearer invisible, summon a storm, and set green wood alight (something which was so uncharacteristically useful that Maddileh had often wondered if the mage who created it had been a knight beforehand); and the Hareskin Pelt, being the hides of four hares magically merged and imbued with an enchantment that would boost other enchantments fourfold when the pelt was wrapped around the item. Both were small and easy to carry and so went into her bag.

It's so hard to know what to take, she thought, moving around the rest of the repository. *Who knows what will be useful in the Gravelands?* It was gradually dawning on her that much of the future came under the category of "who knows," and she wondered how Saralene was faring—a woman who prided herself on planning and foreknowledge. A sharp pain squeezed her heart, making her breathless. *I'm coming for you. I promise.*

It was news to Maddileh that entrances from the living world into the underworld existed outside of the legends; what was even more of a surprise was that there was one so close to the palace. Of course, by horse, it would have been a week's journey, but it was a surprisingly short dragon flight to a wooded hillside, the twin palaces distantly visible.

Maddileh hesitated before the cave opening, hating herself for such cowardice yet unable to forget that many of the worst moments in her life had started out standing in front of a cave. She had every reason to suppose that what lay ahead would be equally terrifying and potentially fatal.

"It's an old dragon's lair, isn't it?" Maddileh said, taking a few cautious steps forward. Mienylyth was already waiting inside the mouth of the tunnel, but even she looked on edge; her tail was lowered, her ears back like those of a cat or dog in distress, and she crouched close to the ground, even though there was plenty of room for her head.

"It is. A place of death for my kind, a place *into* death for your kind. There is much you dir—humans don't know about us sky-riders, and one thing is that our magic can be used to open doorways to other worlds."

"Dragons can simply walk in and out of worlds?" Maddileh asked, impressed.

"No." Mienylyth started down the tunnel, and Maddileh hurried to catch up. "A way into other realms is only possible with blood magic. And a lot of magic is needed, so . . ." The unspoken conclusion lay between them.

Ah.

"What will you do when we return?" Maddileh said in an effort to change the subject. The close confines made her uneasy, and conversation helped to hold back the dread.

"I will fly far away from here. Before I go, I will seek out other dragons, see if they will join me. Company would be welcome. I find myself lonely in my twilight age."

The darkness quickly became absolute. Maddileh dug out a mage orb, but some latent magic in the air sucked all the light away, making it useless. Maddileh was forced to walk with one hand on Mienylyth's hide to navigate. After entering previous dragons' lairs in order to kill them, the irony of walking into one led by a dragon was not lost on Maddileh. The bag of supplies hung awkwardly from her shoulder, banging repeatedly against her hip; she wished fervently for a squire. With the dragon beside her, she couldn't help thinking of pack mules.

"Do not even consider asking," Mienylyth said, startling Maddileh so much the knight jumped.

"Can you read my mind?" Maddileh demanded suspiciously.

"No. Just your face." That wasn't much more reassuring, given the darkness. A childish impulse born of intense anxiety made Maddileh stick her tongue out as far as it would go. Mienylyth's chuckle reverberated down Maddileh's arm and through her body as a cloud of sweet-smelling smoke wafted over her. "I see you can be funny too, little metalwearer."

Upon finally reaching their destination, matters improved when Maddileh found a faintly glowing mage orb lying on the ground that enabled her to see. "Down there," said Mienylyth, pointing to an uneven hole in the ground. The edges were smooth and shiny, like glass that had melted and run, leading Maddileh to think that it might be some kind of natural formation. But when she peered into the hole, she saw rough-hewn steps leading down.

"Is the hole big enough for you to—" Maddileh began before she halted, her cheeks reddening as realisation dawned. Of course Mienylyth would be able to fit down the hole; it had, after all, been created by the melting corpse of a dragon, its gushing blood opening up a way between worlds.

Mienylyth gestured for Maddileh to go first. With a deep, unsteady breath, Maddileh placed her foot on the top step. She expected to feel the ground shift or the world tilt with the momentousness of what she was doing, but there was nothing; she descended the steps into the underworld as easily as she might descend to the training courtyard at the palace.

When she was about thirty steps down, she looked up, wondering how Mienylyth would manage on the narrow staircase. Perhaps she would glide down the central spire. Yet there was no sign of the dragon's bulk above her, and a sudden uncertainty rushed through her. Was this a trap? Revenge? Was something terrible about to—

Something small and warm bumped against her ankle, and she looked down to see a white cat. Peering closer, she discerned patches of scales flashing beneath the fur, and there were tiny wings folded along its back. Its tail had no fur at all, only scales and a pointed tip. The creature looked up, and Maddileh saw two small horn buds on its head.

"I thought perhaps a large dragon at your side would be too noticeable," Mienylyth said.

"Bless the Allfather, but you're adorable!" Maddileh cried, scooping the cat up to examine her closer. Slightly larger than a full-grown cat, the dragon's new body lacked the length and litheness of a cat's body, being stockier, like a bear cub. As she brought it up to her face for a better look, the cat's golden glowing eyes gave her such a baleful stare that Maddileh swiftly returned the cat to the floor. "A most suitable disguise. Very sensible," she said hurriedly before heading down the stairs once more.

As a knight, Maddileh was no stranger to exertion, but as the hours stretched, the journey down the winding steps began to take its toll until each footstep juddered through her bones and her supply bag bruised her hip. When she paused to rest her aching muscles, she looked up to see Mienylyth about two dozen steps behind her, clearly struggling due to her small size. Maddileh watched the dragon for a bit, debating the wisdom of what she was about to do; when the cat was close enough, she picked her up, cradled her in one arm, and continued down. "Just to the bottom of the steps," she said soothingly as the cat struggled. Mienylyth paused, still tense, then settled in Maddileh's grip, although the knight could feel the cat's tail swishing angrily against her side.

When she next stopped, Maddileh found herself idly stroking the cat until Mienylyth growled, deep in her chest, a noise loud enough that it came from a dragon, not a cat.

"Apologies," said Maddileh, desisting. And yet there was something about the little body curled up in her arms that made her spirit feel lighter.

Perhaps this is what Saralene feels for all animals, she mused. The thought of her friend made her heart skip; when she started off again, she walked a little faster.

Just when Maddileh was beginning to think that she would have to sleep on the steps, the end suddenly came in sight. At the bottom was a small cave, not much wider than a person, with a single opening in the wall. Putting the dragon down, Maddileh walked along the passage, which was short and ended at a vast abyss with a stone bridge spanning it.

Beyond that were fields of corn, wheat, and grass, and in the distance, what must have been Findara.

The strength left Maddileh's legs, and she sank to the ground, gazing hollowly at what lay before her. Until now, it hadn't seemed real, and yet here she was. The mage ball flickered, fell to the ground, and then rolled over the edge into the abyss. Maddileh felt that darkness tug at her as if it would suck her down into its depths as well.

"The Perilous Bridge," she murmured, "where all are judged."

FOURTEEN

Saralene spent her first night in Findara listening to tales told at the inn. Many were heroic sagas or personal family stories, designed to delight teller and listener alike. No formal troubadours here—anyone could be a teller of tales. A place was made for her in every gathering she approached, but when she tried to join one particular group in a dark corner, she received hostile looks. Just as she was about to back away, Penn was at her side, saying, "She's new. Let her hear." Amid a few suspicious glances, Saralene sat down and listened. Everyone spoke in whispers about Pravhan's punishments. Besides the pillories, which she'd already witnessed, Saralene heard about the drunkard's cloak: any person found inebriated in the street was to wear a barrel with spikes hammered through it in place of clothes.

She learned how those who repeatedly broke the peace would be forced to exist in the manner of their death. If they'd been sliced open with a sword, their guts would hang out, the skin refusing to knit together. Those who died of a summer fever might spend eternity shivering and sweating, their bodies cold but their skin so sensitive that they cried out in agony if anyone tried to wrap a blanket around them. There was a house on the far side of the city where those who had burned to death were housed, their pitiful cries echoing down empty streets where no one could bear to reside.

Each story contained one common element: the empty guards. Pravhan either couldn't find any humans to act as his enforcers or else didn't trust anyone to do so, and thus had created a cohort of invisible creatures that wore armour and couldn't be resisted. Anyone who tried to fight against them found themselves grappling with mere air while an empty gauntlet dragged them to their doom.

Eventually, Saralene left the group, feeling dizzy and sick with all she'd learned. She had hoped it would be a simple thing to seek out Pravhan and ask him to carve a way back into the world of the living. If he needed persuading, she had the serpentstone necklace that she could offer him; surely, she reasoned, that was why Mienylyth had insisted she take it. But she'd been counting on Pravhan being a merciful man; that was certainly what all the stories said. Wise, just, and merciful, someone who would understand her need to get back to the living world and help the fourteen realms. Yet now she was learning new stories that told of a ruthless, maybe even vindictive, ruler, hardly the sort of man who would take pity on a High Mage. Especially not one, she thought, who'd already cheated death once.

When a new day dawned and Penn opened the doors, Saralene set off, determined to see the truth of Findara for herself. To her shock, it wasn't long before she came across a living testament of the stories she'd heard: a man walking down the street, his spindly legs staggering under the weight of the barrel he carried. Two strips of cloth attached to the barrel lay over his shoulders, the skin raw and bruised around the edges, making her wonder how long he'd been carrying it. His legs were marred by blood, with fresh rivulets running over what was already crusted on his skin; every movement made him wince as the spikes inside mercilessly pricked his flesh.

Wading through the backstreets, she came across a woman balancing a bundle of washing on her shoulder rather than on her hip because at her side was a cloth bag that contained her stomach and liver. The woman winced with every step; her face was haggard, her arms bony. Saralene shuddered as they passed each other, thinking what it must be like to eat food and then see it pass through your stomach on the outside of your body. Petros, no doubt, would have approached the woman and asked to observe such a unique, disquieting event, but Saralene said nothing, unwilling to disturb her misery.

Saralene found the street of burn victims but couldn't bring herself to venture closer than the last occupied house. Their cries, even from such a distance, were too distressing. As she turned to walk back the way she'd come, she found people stepping aside to let a group of armed men through, and Saralene got her first look at the empty guards. All that was visible was armour—helmets, gauntlets, shoulder pads, breastplates, greaves—with nothing connecting them but air. The ambiguity was truly chilling: Was there a being trapped in there? A mind? Or was the armour merely moving under enchantment? She was not sorry to see the back of them when they disappeared into the unoccupied parts of the city. Presumably, with no ears, the sounds of torment did not bother them.

As Saralene stopped to eat a midday meal, she was racked with doubt. *If this is what Pravhan's kingdom is like, what is*

C'sava's like? It must be awful if it's to be worse than this. And how can this be where the good people go? How is this a just afterlife?

Packing her food away, she noticed with alarm just how loose the skin around her wrists had become. She tugged at it, her stomach flipping to see how it sagged; the same was true under her arms.

The doleful sound of a bell broke through her panicked thoughts, and she saw everyone in the street beyond start to hurry off in the same direction. Saralene joined them, observing pinched and worried faces on either side of her. Ahead, a tall figure joined the crowd and, recognising Penn, Saralene caught her up. "What's going on?"

"There you are, duck," Penn said, seizing her hand; the comfort of another's touch was so overwhelming it brought tears to Saralene's eyes. "You stay with me. I'll see you right."

"But where are we going?"

"To the Prince's palace. That was a summons. A punishment is to be meted out."

To her astonishment, Saralene realised that the palace, which had seemed so distant during her wanderings, was now looming ahead of her. The front doors were massive, allowing at least a dozen people abreast in. Swept along by a crowd that knew where it was going, Saralene had little time to take in the majesty of the corridor before she found herself in a huge room with three levels of balconies and a large floor space in front of a stage. To the left of the stage was an ornate stone throne in which Prince Pravhan was seated, straight-backed and with an imperious expression. As the hall filled, a woman was brought out by two guards to stand in the middle of the stage, her head bowed and her hands shackled.

"Tilla!" The voice from the crowd was hoarse, panicked. Even though it seemed everyone was packed tightly, nevertheless a gap opened up to allow the man who'd shouted over to the stage. He climbed up and embraced the girl. Pravhan didn't move, didn't even seem to notice this incursion.

Saralene would never have believed a gathering of so many people could be so silent if she hadn't witnessed it for herself. And the air—which should have been full of the odours of so many bodies—was dry and dusty. When all was still, Pravhan got up from his throne and walked towards the two people on the stage. He was tall with tight-fitting black clothes that emphasised his sinewy physique, except for his coat, which flared behind him when he moved. His skin was pale—bloodless. His shirt was high-necked, almost to his chin, a curiously feminine style.

Standing to one side, he said solemnly, "Dolomere Harst, your daughter is charged with the crime of crossing realms. You are charged as her accomplice." Dolomere wrapped his arms more tightly around his daughter, shaking with silent sobs. Tilla stood as she had so far: head down, motionless.

Pravhan addressed the assembly. "You all know that judgment on the Perilous Bridge is absolute. If you are assigned to one realm, you cannot cross to reside in the other. That would be unjust." His eyes swept the crowd before him; when his gaze passed over Saralene, she shuddered.

"Tilla Harst was consigned to my brother's realm, and yet she sought to reside in mine." Without turning, he pointed at her. "Witness now what happens to those who disobey the laws."

Onto the stage were pushed five stone sarcophagi; the last two had their lids wide open while the others had lids in varying degrees of closure. From at least one of them came desperate moaning. Four guards separated father and daughter. Dolomere fought, shrieking and trying to get free; the guards had to haul him bodily to the farthest tomb.

"They're going to—" Saralene whispered urgently, but Penn silenced her with a glare. Everyone was mute and staring at the stage. This wasn't the bloodlust of a bullbaiting or the excitement of a tourney; it was an atmosphere of numb observation. Here, Saralene realised, was another of the inn's stories being played out—the slowly closing tomb that sealed the condemned inside in agonisingly incremental amounts.

Tilla didn't resist being led to the stone tomb, but when the guard gestured she should get in, she shied away. Then she too was being manhandled into the sarcophagus, shouting out pleas and apologies. It made no difference.

Once the two wrongdoers were in the tombs, the lids started to lower. Saralene's stomach lurched. They really were going to seal them in alive. Except they weren't really alive, were they? Did that make the punishment greater or lesser? The dead weren't supposed to feel pain, but then she thought of the stories of those forced to live with the injuries of their deaths and the agonies they suffered.

The lids did not close all the way but left enough of a gap so those inside could put out a hand or arm, which both Dolomere and Tilla did. The distance between the coffins was fractionally too much for them to touch fingers, a deliberate positioning, Saralene suspected.

They'll be trapped like that for how long? Forever? They'll be able to see each other through the openings but not touch. And slowly, slowly, they'll be cut off from each other and the world forever as the lids close. Saralene felt the food she'd eaten threaten to come back up.

As the sarcophagi were wheeled away, Pravhan spoke again. "Peace comes with rules. Peace requires justice. Those who seek to disturb the peace will be punished. Those who seek to flee their assigned realm will be punished." His eyes had been sweeping across the crowd, but now they came to rest in one spot—on Saralene. "Those who think to cheat the right order of things and leave the Gravelands entirely will be punished. Now, go about your business." He walked off the stage, and the room was filled with the shuffling of many feet as everyone left.

Swept along with the crowd once more, Saralene's mind was full of dread. Pravhan had stated publicly that he would not help her. That meant C'sava was her only chance. Yet if Pravhan was ruthless, what would the ruler of the Night City be like? She remembered Luciel's advice not to form preconceptions and hoped she might still find a way out of this. She had meant it when she said it was better for her to die than let Hosh rule again, but even a day in Findara was proving just how precarious life after death could be.

As she stepped back out into the daylight, Saralene grasped the serpentstone pendant that lay beneath her clothes. Her fingertips felt puffy and clumsy with the extra layer of skin that was forming on them.

Please hurry, Maddileh.

FIFTEEN

A TRAVELER'S GUIDE TO CUSTOMS IN THE FOURTEEN REALMS
Chapter 11

Much like Birth Customs (Chapter 3) and Marriage Ceremonies (Chapter 7), the death rites observed are mostly the same across the fourteen realms, with a few regional variations. Key differences to note are:

In the Fourteenth Realm, there is no burial, only cremation, due to the Zombie Court legend which, while discredited, still holds sway in the minds of the common people.

In the Sixth Realm, black dogs are bred specially for funerals and released onto the street. It is believed that the dog is a guide to the Gravelands and so will conduct the soul there before returning home. If it does not return home, then the departed soul is deemed lost and condemned to wander as a ghost. Incidentally, when a black dog dies, specific funeral rites are accorded to it (see Appendix 6).

In the Eleventh Realm, the family of the deceased are bidden to silence until the funeral is over. Although these days it is seen as a mark of respect, the custom arises from the idea that the departed soul would linger by its body if it heard a word. If it saw an open mouth, it would leap inside the body (see Yaraini, the Woman With Her Brother's Soul).

As at births and weddings, food is crucial at these times. In all fourteen realms, an edible gift must be presented when calling at a house of mourning, to ensure that the living are well-fed in their grief and the dead are offered sustenance in the afterlife. However, the wrong gift can cause huge offence, so care must be taken.

Flowers are an acceptable alternative, but they must not be white, as white flowers are associated with the Night City.

Each realm (and, most likely, many regions within each realm) will have its own variation of gravefood. However, a common theme is that nothing living or fresh must be used in the making of such food. For example, raisins and prunes are permitted, as they are seen as decayed and dead. But fresh fruit like blackcurrants and strawberries are not. Eggs may be used only if they've not been laid next to a fertilised egg and must have been kept in a dark place for at least three days (to mimic, it's believed, a tomb).

Nuts are acceptable both as ingredients or as a gift on their own since their wrinkled skin gives them the air of something aged and dead.

There is one exception to the fresh ingredients rule: anything harvested from beneath the ground, such as potatoes, parsnips, or carrots. This is because things beneath the earth encroach on the realm of the Bloodless Princes and therefore are acceptable offerings.

Bread can be offered, but only unleavened. Fresh bread using yeast should only be used as an offering to the Bloodless Princes because the yeast is dead at the start, revivified in the rising dough, and then killed in the oven. This process of resurrection and death is appropriate only to the Princes.

Sixteen

Never had anything taken so much courage as Maddileh's first steps onto that bridge. Technically, she wasn't dead, and so should not meet with judgment as she crossed; and even if she did, Maddileh felt she'd led a mostly blameless life and should be admitted to the Peaceful City. But doubt was ever present in every human mind. *Have I really lived a good life? If Maddileh was cast down into the abyss and then sent to live in C'sava's realm, how would she find Saralene?*

"My understanding of humans," said Mienylyth ahead of her, "is that to warn you not to look down would be counterproductive."

"Yes. Very." It was hard to force the words through gritted teeth. It appeared that the dragon was trotting merrily across the bridge with all the grace of her assumed form, but Maddileh could not be absolutely sure because her eyes were fixed firmly on Findara. Shifting her gaze away might draw it to the abyss.

About halfway across, an agonised scream drifted up from below, and the strength left Maddileh's legs. She fell forward with a cry, landing facedown on the narrow bridge, her palms stinging with the impact. The supply bag slid from her shoulder to her elbow where it swung over the chasm, like a pendulum keeping time. Maddileh tried to dig her fingernails into stone.

Mienylyth sat down in front of her, tail swishing. "If you can sit up, I can help."

"A moment," Maddileh gasped. It was, in fact, several moments before she found the courage to lever herself up even a bit. Mienylyth walked forward and rubbed her head against Maddileh's. The gesture had always irritated Maddileh with real cats, but right now, it was the most comforting thing in the world. As she straightened unsteadily, kneeling on the bridge, Mienylyth curled up on her lap, gentle vibrations from her soft purrs traveling through Maddileh's body, unknotting tense muscles.

Picking the dragon up in her arms, Maddileh stood up unsteadily and adjusted the bag. The drop now seemed no worse than that from a greased log at the summer fair. The bridge was not narrow but perfectly proportioned, and she walked forward with ease. When she got to the other side, Mienylyth jumped down, and immediately Maddileh's body fell victim to violent shakes and she was once again on her knees. She remained that way until the shaking subsided, and then she looked up to see a beautiful woman standing before her, the beads on the ends of her braids winking with light as she leaned down to help Maddileh up.

"Greetings, Maddileh," said Luciel with a smile like a sun. "I believe a friend of yours passed this way just recently. I wish I could invite you to my home and hear word of the world above, but time is not your friend here. I told Saralene that the longer she spends here, the less chance she has of getting out. More than three days and her skin will shed like a snake and she'll be stuck here. You too."

Maddileh gaped at Luciel, then glared at the dragon. "Why didn't you tell me this?"

Mienylyth's feline shoulders gave a little shrug. "I did not know it. I am infinitely wise in my own kind, but my knowledge is more limited for egg-crackers. There is no such rule for the Peregrinate."

"That's the dragon underworld," Luciel supplied when Maddileh looked blank. "But before you go, I can give you two gifts. This waterskin contains water from my stream. You will find that no water from the living world can survive here. And this is a gem that holds a sliver of the Gravelands's daylight. The first I know will aid you; whether you use the second I will leave to your judgment when the time comes. Now, hurry."

Luciel put a hand on Maddileh's lower back and gently propelled her forward. Maddileh had time to mumble her thanks, awed and confused by the encounter before Luciel was walking back up the hill to her home. For a brief moment, Maddileh thought she saw a man standing in the doorway of the house, but an instant later, he was gone, and she couldn't be sure her unsettled mind hadn't imagined it.

Maddileh and Mienylyth traveled in silence, the knight overwhelmed by all she had experienced in a few short hours. Walking beneath a sky of churning clouds did not help her sense of balance either. They had covered only half the distance to the city before fatigue claimed her and she sank down to the ground.

"Need to eat," she muttered by way of explanation as Mienylyth walked back. However, rooting around in the supplies bag brought a nasty surprise: a third of her food had crumbled to ash. "What's this?" Maddileh said, her hands grey and dusty.

Mienylyth sniffed the bag. "Interesting. What have you lost?"

After a swift stocktaking, Maddileh said, "The apples, cheese, bread—except the flatbread." She opened up some onion and apple pastries she'd brought; inside, the onion was still there, but the other ingredients were dust. She groaned. "Even the oatcakes are gone. All that's left are nuts and the gravefood." There was logic here, but Maddileh couldn't distinguish it through her weariness. Luckily, Mienylyth was more astute.

"You have lost the fresher items. Your grave offerings only contain dried fruit, nuts, flour, dark eggs, yes? That is why they remain. Evidently, the food of the dead is the only food that can be consumed here."

Maddileh groaned again. Not knowing what she might be able to eat in the Gravelands, she'd packed enough food to last her a week. But this setback left her with rations for only a few days, with nothing extra to barter with if she needed to. Checking the other parts of her bag, she became more frantic. Not only was the food duplication potion gone, but so were the Trinity Ring and the Hareskin Pelt.

"Your trinkets have gone too, yes?"

"They weren't trinkets, they were . . . But yes." She narrowed her eyes. "Did you know that would happen too?"

"No, but I surmised a little while ago. Your light-globe fell into the abyss the moment we entered the Gravelands. It seemed sensible that no human magic could survive here; otherwise, your mages would surely rule the dead, yes?"

Now I will definitely have to give up the Blade, Maddileh thought wretchedly. Of course, there was no question that Saralene was far more important than a mere sword, yet up until that moment, Maddileh had harboured hopes that perhaps she might be able to tempt the Prince with something different.

"The Resurrection Dish is still here," she said flatly.

"Dragon magic seems unaffected by your underworld," Mienylyth said. Then, in a surprisingly sympathetic voice, she added, "At least you have water too."

Maddileh spent the next few minutes dusting as much ash off the remaining food as she could before nibbling a grave cake. It sated her hunger but made her teeth ache with the sweetness.

Allfather's balls—nothing but gravefood? I'm going to be dreaming of sausages. She washed away the cloying sweetness with the water, which was cold and refreshing.

When they finally arrived at the gates of Findara, the light was beginning to change. The clouds were clearing from the sky to show a blanket of stars, and a feeling of twilight was definitely present around them. Maddileh reached into her bag, intending to take out the sunstone that Luciel had given her. Perhaps it was a way to keep the Night City at bay when darkness fell, but there was a sudden pressure on her shoulder as Mienylyth jumped up.

"Don't," the dragon said. "I don't think Luciel gave us that light-star just for illumination. She said to use your judgment, and I judge that right now is not the moment. Instead, we should get under cover as quickly as we can. This place smells wrong, like roses in winter or rotting meat in a fresh egg. Let us find your heart-mate. Her magical knowledge will no doubt prove invaluable. Her skin-scent is strong. Follow me."

Mienylyth jumped off and scampered away at a surprisingly fast pace. The streets got steadily emptier as they progressed, and Maddileh began to feel distinctly uneasy. By the time they turned a corner and finally saw Saralene heading towards an open doorway, the dread Maddileh felt was so great that the sight of her friend seemed to both swell and shatter her heart. With a cry, and without thinking, Maddileh raced forward and swept the mage into her arms, kissing her full on the mouth. She enjoyed the sensation of soft lips on hers for less than a heartbeat before embarrassment overcame her and she hastily pulled back, wiping her mouth as if she could wipe away her impetuous mistake just as easily. *I am her friend. Her Champion. Not her lover. I don't even know if she . . . if I could . . .*

"Quickly, we must get inside," Mienylyth said urgently, darting through the nearby door. Maddileh looked at Saralene, who looked composed if a little dazed.

"Your cat is right," Saralene said. "Inside. We can discuss everything in there." Only as they were hurrying towards the door did Saralene seem to grasp what she'd just said. Frowning, she asked, "Your *cat*?"

Saralene's lips still tingled with the warmth of that kiss. In truth, it had not been how she'd imagined it would be—too hard and fast—yet it had been full of passion. But what did it mean that Maddileh had wiped it away? Did she regret it? Then why did she do it in the first place?

Sighing, Saralene slumped back in her chair. There were more important things to concentrate on. Now that Maddileh was here—and Mienylyth too, if in a somewhat surprising form—they could proceed to the Night City and see if C'sava would cut them a way back to the living world with the Fireborne Blade. From what she'd seen in the Peaceful City, Pravhan might not be as kindly disposed towards her plight as she'd hoped. She felt it wise to investigate the Night City before making her next move. Yet despite the urgency she felt as her time here ticked down to eternity, she didn't want to go to the Night City tonight. She needed Maddileh and Mienylyth to see the Peaceful City; she needed to know if they were as unnerved by it all as she was. The place nagged at her like a rotten tooth that needed to be pulled.

So, when Maddileh said that they should approach Pravhan as soon as the door was unbolted, Saralene said, "I don't think he's the Prince we need."

Maddileh had scowled at her but not argued. The knight was already in a bad mood; her eyes had lit up when Penn had produced a bowl of onion soup and dark flatbreads, but at the first taste, she had spat out a mouthful of ash. It seemed that Maddileh couldn't stomach the food of the dead, and when Mienylyth had pointed out that gravefood from the world of the living was edible, Penn had hurried off and then returned with a large slice of parsnip cake and a few squares of gingerbread. "What the living offer at our resting places makes its way to us. This was baked by my granddaughter, I think. It's a little dry, but I would be humbled if the bearer of the Fireborne Blade would be able to eat it." Maddileh had thanked her and eaten it, but it was clear (to Saralene at least) that the food was not to her taste.

I'm going to have to feed her a whole table's worth of onion tarts when we return to make up for this. Saralene had consumed a slice of cheese pie, which she tried not to eat with too much relish in front of Maddileh, and a small cup of potato wine, which Maddileh had at least been able to drink as well, although it didn't stop her complaining about the rest of her meal.

Saralene's arrival had caused little interest, but tonight, there was lots of excited chatter and many expectant glances at Maddileh. A real knight with a famous sword and a horned cat must have a wealth of stories, and Saralene could tell the patrons were going to claim Maddileh the moment she finished eating. She wasn't wrong, and as Maddileh settled herself in front of a sea of expectant faces, Saralene was grateful to have some time to figure out what she was going to say to her friend.

Mienylyth jumped onto the table next to her. "Are you well, magic-worker?"

"I am. But I feel . . . drawn out. Depleted."

The dragon was watching her with an uncomfortably intense stare. "We spoke to Luciel. She told us of the time limit that applies to your existence. We should make haste to the ruler of this realm and see this thing done."

After a pause, Saralene asked, "What do you think of this world, Mienylyth?"

The dragon sat still a moment, her scaled tail twitching. "There is a wrongness here. A canker."

"I think it stems from the ruler."

"Can you fix it?" the dragon asked.

"I don't know."

"Then forget it," Mienylyth said bluntly.

"I can't! This place is the last destination for all humans. If I can use my magic to fix it—"

"Your magic works here?" Mienylyth said sharply.

"Yes."

"The magical items we brought with us turned to dust."

"Allmother save us! But wait, I saw the Fireborne Blade, so—"

"All the *human* magical items. Your flying-lights. The potions and artefacts. The Blade was not made by humans, and so it still works here."

"I thought it was made by the Dragon Smith."

Mienylyth paused, considering. "He was human, true. But the Blade was forged from our earth-ribbons, heated by our fire, and kissed by your Death. It transcends such petty magics as you work. It is possible that your magic still works because of the dragon magic in your blood and the serpentstone against your heart. But that is only guesswork. We should not rely on it. We should get you to the prince of this realm swiftly."

"Not this realm. We must go into the Night City."

"Oh?"

"Pravhan is . . . not merciful. He will not allow us to leave. Our only hope is with C'sava."

"Then we should go now, while it is dark."

"No. Tomorrow night. Give me one day to show Maddileh what is wrong with this place."

The dragon gave her a hard stare, then offered a feline shrug. "It is your time you are wasting. I have no objections. Now, excuse me. I must see to my own nourishment." She leaped gracefully off the table and went to sit by Maddileh, soaking up the words.

Next morning, Maddileh was still hopeful that Pravhan would help them, but Saralene said, "Give me just a morning to show you why I don't think he will. What harm can a morning do?" Maddileh had looked at her assessingly then, and Saralene knew that she was taking in the way that the skin was loose around her neck, how her hair looked lank and flat. Even her fine clothes looked ragged. "Just the morning. It's important."

"All right, then."

They asked questions of the stallholders, and if any proved uncommunicative, Mienylyth would leap onto a spot nearby and start to purr. Mesmerised by the creature, the person would talk, their words coming out as if in a daze. Saralene wondered if it was dragon magic or just nostalgia for lost pets that loosened their tongues.

They heard about the sarcophagus punishment, used mostly on families. Saralene learned a new story about a labyrinth that was meant to have a single way out, only no one had ever found it; grotesque, hungry creatures stalked its passages, devouring anyone before they could locate the exit.

They went to see the finger pillories, the bloody dancers, and the woman with her innards in a bag. Maddileh had stared at the woman and then quickly away, her throat working convulsively. After that, they tracked down the street of the burned. The screams and moans were enough for Saralene, but Maddileh insisted on going inside one of the houses; she came out again an unhealthy green colour, staggered to the wall, leaned against it, then slowly slid to the ground where she sat, staring at nothing.

"Your underworld is as rotting as a corpse," said Mienylyth, her tail flicking unhappily. Wisps of smoke curled up from her nose until she sneezed. "I can see why you think a ruler who imposes such punishments would not be amenable to our cause. We must seek out the other brother."

Maddileh nodded, her eyes staring into the distance. She didn't say another word, even when they were back at the inn. She merely took a cup of ale and sat staring into the flames of the fire.

They ate in silence when food was served; Maddileh didn't even wince at the sweetness of the grave cake she was eating. When they were done, Mienylyth said, "It's time," and the three of them headed for the door. But Penn was there before them, blocking the way.

"Are you mad? You can't go out there."

"We're not mad, and we must," said Saralene, reaching past her. Penn batted her hand away.

"You'll let them in," she protested.

Maddileh drew the Blade. Silence descended. "I will not let them pass inside," she vowed.

Penn eyed the sword then darted forward and picked up Mienylyth. "Well, you're not taking this poor little thing. They'll roast it and eat it."

"Take heed, dirt-walker. I'm not a sly-eyes but a sky-rider—desist!" But Penn couldn't hear her. As Maddileh stepped forward, Mienylyth shot a burst of flame that singed the doorjamb, and Penn dropped her with a scream.

Maddileh scooped up Mienylyth and perched the dragon on her shoulder. "The cat comes with us," she said resolutely.

The sound of the bolts being drawn and the latch lifted was the loudest noise in the room. The three of them stepped outside and closed the door. There was a moment's pause before the muffled sound of the bolts swiftly sliding back on the other side.

SEVENTEEN

Maddileh hadn't been sure what to expect from the Night City, but certainly not moonlight and silver flowers. Like the daytime, there was no obvious light source, just a diffuse glow and a sky of stars above. But on what had been bare walls there were now lush green creepers with white flowers blooming on them. "What are they?" she asked, entranced.

"I don't know, but probably best to avoid them," Saralene replied.

"This way," Mienylyth said, starting off down the street.

Maddileh and Saralene exchanged glances before following.

"How do you know?" the knight asked as they caught up.

"I can sense a presence. One I know well."

"Here?" Saralene asked. "Who?"

"Let me say only when I've been proved right," Mienylyth said, and Maddileh rolled her eyes.

For a city that was supposed to hold the unrighteous dead, Maddileh had expected something more sinister. But Findara by night simply felt like a gloomier version of the Peaceful City. The streets were clean and mostly empty, the only hint of decay being the odd patch of mushrooms they came across growing from the floor. The walls were almost entirely covered with creepers, like ivy and the white-flowered plant; such vegetation had been lacking in Pravhan's realm, and here it gave the streets an appealing natural quality, making the Peaceful City seem almost sterile by contrast. When they did pass people in the street, Maddileh's hand twitched towards her sword hilt, but the passersby merely nodded at them if they noticed them at all.

"Not what I was expecting," Maddileh whispered.

Saralene nodded, her eyes wide as she looked around.

Maddileh noticed that the dragon would give the mushrooms a wide berth, and she was going to ask why until she saw a decaying human hand sticking out of the end of one pile, a delicate fungus growing from the fingertips. Repugnance twisted her stomach.

It wasn't long before they turned into a little alleyway. Sitting on a wooden chair in the alley, smoking a pipe, was a tall, thin man who stood up when he saw them. The leather apron and the scars on his arms gave him away as a blacksmith. He looked like he was going to greet them, but then he saw the cat and beamed.

"Mienylyth! I never thought . . . A dragon! Here!" The man's face was grimy with soot, but now tears were tracking pale lines down his cheeks. He picked up the dragon and held her lovingly to his chest. To Maddileh's surprise, Mienylyth closed her eyes and, in a most catlike fashion, rubbed her head against the man's chin.

"Smith. It warms my heart to see you."

"You're the Dragon Smith," Saralene said, slightly faster on the uptake than Maddileh.

"I am," said the man, putting the dragon down. "And you must be the mage and the knight I was sent to accompany."

"Who sent you?"

"Prince C'sava, of course." He started off down the alley,

Mienylyth trotting unconcernedly behind; Maddileh and Saralene had no choice but to follow.

"How did the Prince know we were here? Or that we had a dragon with us?"

"His Highness has his sources," Smith said enigmatically.

A thought struck Maddileh. "Luciel. I saw a man in her garden."

"Why are you here?" Saralene asked. "You are a good man. A hero." She paused, then said awkwardly, "Is it because of the dragons?"

Smith paused before saying, "I started out in the Peaceful City, certainly. But you have been there. You have seen Pravhan's concept of justice. Of order. His methods didn't appeal to me, and so I crossed over."

"And Prince C'sava hasn't punished you?"

"No. He punishes no one who crosses. That fact alone should tell you much. The old distinctions of one city for the good, one for the wicked is redundant now. Humans are not as they were in the time of the Bloodless Princes—violent, rash. The living world breeds better people. And besides, the Night City was never about punishment—only containment. The living world has changed for the better—I don't see why the Gravelands can't do the same." Smith glanced back at them. "Prince Pravhan is not a man easily swayed by argument. Despite his reputation, our Prince is more open-minded."

They were on a longer street now, with more people. Some of them were staggering, clearly drunk. A couple were even fighting. Stalls with fresh food lined one side of the street with people merely helping themselves. It seemed unruly, but not terrible.

Maddileh had only seen Findara's palace from a distance, but as they drew close, Saralene said, "It's exactly the same."

Smith smiled. "Of course. It's the same city both day and night."

"Where do you go during the day?" Maddileh asked as they crossed a bridge leading to two large doors.

"I'm sorry?" Smith asked.

"Well, at night, the Peaceable shut themselves away, barring the door so that the Nighters roaming the street can't get in. So where do the Nighters go when it's day?"

"Nowhere," said Smith, heading not towards the ornate main doors but a small, normal-size one to the right of them. "The cities exist side by side, always. It is only the Princes who cannot exist in the same space—one exists solely at night, the other during the day. If Pravhan is telling people that they cannot go outside at night, I think that plays more to his own ends of terror and control than anything else."

"But we crossed realms by stepping outside during the night," Saralene said.

Smith sighed. "I don't know all the secrets of this world. You'd best get His Highness to explain. Now, please step inside. He'll be waiting."

"Is he trustworthy?" Saralene asked.

Looking embarrassed, Smith said, "I am but a humble—"

"Speak!" Mienylyth said sharply. "You are wiser than all gem-stealers I know. Present company excepted," she added hastily. Smith looked up at the starry sky, evidently contemplating his answer.

"You should trust him as much as you trust any prince," he said eventually.

"Which is not at all," Mienylyth muttered.

With an amused grin, Smith added, "But you should trust him more than his brother." And with a swift bow, he was gone.

The fort where Maddileh had grown up had seemed grand when she was a child. Living in the palace had taught her the true meaning of luxury. But the Prince's residence made the High Mage's home seem cramped and dull. Three dragons could have stood on top of each other and not hit their heads on the ceiling. The floors were made of marble polished to such a sheen they were almost mirrors. No tapestries or paintings hung on these walls either, but the carvings on the stonework were decoration enough.

With no guide waiting, Saralene led the way to the audience chamber she remembered from Pravhan's castle, and sure enough, there was C'sava waiting for them. He had eschewed the throne, instead sitting on a chair that had been placed centrally on the main stage, a serene smile on his face.

Time to see if we're going home, Maddileh thought.

Saralene was shocked. Of course, the mythology stated the Princes were twins, but all the depictions of C'sava in books and paintings had him as twisted and leering, sallow-skinned and cruel. Yet the man who stood before her was identical to Pravhan: tall; slick dark hair; pale skin but fine cheekbones. He too wore dark clothes, but his shirt was open at the neck to reveal the wound that had killed him.

C'sava also held himself more easily than Pravhan, who had stood straight as a spear, his expression cold and regal. In contrast, C'sava appeared relaxed and even smiled as he descended the stage to meet them, although it was clearly a political smile rather than a genuine one.

"Welcome to my realm, Saralene, Maddileh, and"—he glanced at Mienylyth—"cat."

"This is Mienylyth," Maddileh said, "although I suspect you already know that."

"I knew not her name. You are welcome too." Mienylyth regarded him with a remarkable imitation of feline indifference and blew out a puff of smoke. Turning his attention back to the two women, C'sava said, "I believe you have something you wish to ask me."

"If you already know what we are going to ask, do we need to?" Saralene said. This felt too rehearsed, almost as if he was manoeuvering them.

C'sava gave them a shrug that would have looked more at home on a rogue than a prince. "If you don't ask for what you want, I can't ask for what I want."

"And what do you want?"

"The Fireborne Blade." His answer was so blunt that she was momentarily taken aback.

Glancing at Maddileh, she saw defensiveness but no surprise.

You knew he was going to ask for it.

"That is a costly gift," Saralene said carefully. "Is there nothing else we can offer you instead? We possess—"

"Your friend will tell you," C'sava interrupted, "that her attempt to bring magical items into the Gravelands failed."

Maddileh looked guiltily at Saralene and said, "I brought the Trinity Ring and the Hareskin Pelt, and they both crumbled to dust in my bag. I'm so sorry."

Saralene felt lightheaded with how badly this was going. Maddileh had lost *two* of the most valued museum exhibits? She tried to push such worries aside and turned back to C'sava. She drew a breath to offer up the serpentstone, but Mienylyth hissed at her. C'sava chuckled.

"I believe your dragon is warning you against offering the Resurrection Bowl. I do not want it, but I have to advise that it will do you no good here. If you cannot get out, what good is being alive? Already I see our world eating at your flesh. You would have to be reborn over and over and over again."

Saralene touched her cheek where she could feel her outer skin peeling away. "Why do you want the Blade?" she asked.

"I want it to kill my brother." Taking in Maddileh's horrified expression, his eyes gleamed. "When Smith forged it, he asked me to imbue the Blade with Death's kiss. I did so, while whispering a promise that it would one day return to me. It has done its service in the human world, and now it must fulfil the other part of its purpose. I only made it so that I could one day use it to kill Pravhan. Give me the sword and this disparate realm will be united under one ruler." He gave Saralene a searching look. "You have seen the extent of my brother's madness. The whole of Findara is tainted by him and his punishments."

"Are you jealous that he has taken over your role as punisher?" Maddileh said, needling.

C'sava sighed. "You should know better than to believe what you read. The Night City was meant for the undesirables, yes, but not to be punished by me. If you explored my city further, you would find that Findara metes out its own punishments to the unworthy. My role is simply to rule, to keep order. My citizens fear the city, not me. But Pravhan's subjects . . ." He left the conclusion in thought only.

"But how will you kill him?" Maddileh said. "You can't both exist at the same time. Or did the stories get that wrong too?"

"No, that is correct. Daylight and moonlight effect the switch—when one changes to the other, so our rules and our bodies switch. But I believe, knight, that you have in your bag something that will shift the balance in my favour."

"The sunstone," Mienylyth said. "It holds the sunlight of this place. Placed in Pravhan's presence at nightfall, the two states will exist at the same time, and both brothers can exist in the same place."

"There is nothing so sharp as the mind of a dragon," C'sava said, sounding genuinely impressed. Then his manner turned earnest as he added, "If you don't trust my word, then think on the fact that Luciel gave you that stone. She believes I alone would make a better ruler than my brother. If you cannot trust *me*, will you trust her? Or trust the truth that you see with your own eyes?" C'sava spread his hands wide and smiled. "If you help me remove my brother, I promise I shall release you from this realm."

Saralene had spent too long in politics to miss a vaguely worded promise when she met one. "That's not good enough. Promise specifically you will use the Blade to cut a way between worlds and send us home."

"A mind like a dragon," C'sava said. Mienylyth gave a little smoky snort. "Very well. I will use the Blade to cut a way between worlds and release you from my realm. Now, do we have a bargain?"

After exchanging a glance with Maddileh, Saralene said, "We shall think on it."

All the good humour fled from C'sava's face; in a tone of irritation, he said, "Don't think too long." He brought his hands together with a boom as loud as a thunderclap, and the three of them were back in the Dragon's Eye, the patrons backing away in shock.

Penn looked from one to the other. "How did you . . . The door . . ." She clamped her mouth shut, turned away, and busied herself with cleaning a table. The rest of the room followed suit, some of them shifting their stools so that their backs were firmly to the three of them. Looking at Saralene, Maddileh said, "I suggest we start thinking about it right now."

After an hour, Maddileh's stomach was still unsettled and sore from the violent effects of the transportation spell. Saralene had seemed unfazed by it, and Maddileh prayed that was because of her familiarity with magic and not due to the degradation of her flesh. Her skin looked almost translucent in places now and, most worryingly, a piece of dead skin had fallen out of her sleeve while they were talking. It was clear to Maddileh that the woman she loved was close to being lost, and that made the situation urgent and their inability to reach a decision frustrating.

"The evidence in C'sava's favour is compelling," Saralene admitted. "Both Luciel—whom we trust—and Smith— whom Mienylyth trusts—believe he would be a better ruler."

"And his city smells better than this one," Mienylyth said.

"The question is not whether he will make a good ruler but merely a better one," Saralene added.

"Yes, but—" Maddileh began, but Mienylyth interrupted.

"No. The real question here is do you wish to return to the land of the living? I have let you talk it out in the hope you might reach a decision by yourselves, but the truth is that the Blade must be in Death's hands before it will cut through realms. So, we must side with C'sava, the only prince who has said he will use it for such."

"We could at least *ask* Pravhan," Maddileh insisted. "He might agree as well."

"I need a drink," Saralene said wearily, standing up and heading to the bar. When everybody ignored her, she walked to the other side and served herself.

"I feel we are unwelcome here," Mienylyth commented, looking around.

"We are rule breakers," Maddileh replied. "We know how Pravhan deals with those who cross realms, and I imagine such punishment awaits us if we get caught. They"—she gestured around them—"keep away out of self-preservation."

"And knowing this, you still wish to approach Pravhan and ask for his aid?" Maddileh had no answer to that. After a moment's silence, Mienylyth said softly, "You do, of course, know of another way to breach realms."

"I do?" Hope flared inside the knight.

"The way we came in. We cannot return that way," Mienylyth added hastily, "since doors in the underworld only work in one direction. But the same method could be used to gain an exit. Had you considered that?"

Realisation dawned, and Maddileh's stomach soured further. Coldly, she said, "I had not."

Mienylyth cocked her head, an ear twitching. "No, I see you had not," she said in a tone of mild surprise.

In a flash of anger, Maddileh picked the dragon up by the scruff of her neck and held her up to her face, staring into those golden eyes. Her voice was as steel. "I have learned a lot, dragon, in our time together, and I feel I know you better. But I see that you haven't grown to know me at all if you believe I would ever countenance such cruelty. I will not sacrifice one friend for another." Mienylyth, who had been squirming, stilled at that. Maddileh lowered her gently to the table, then smoothed down the fur she had ruffled.

"Friend?" Mienylyth said. "I am chastened. I set a test before you, and I see now that I was wrong. I should have listened to my own heart that believed you would not consider such a thing—and I did so believe. But I have long mistrusted humans, and it is a hard habit to break. I am sorry . . . my friend."

Saralene returned then, and although she clearly sensed that something had taken place, she did not ask what it was. Instead, they fell back to debating how to proceed. Mienylyth maintained her stolidly logical stance that they needed to acquiesce to C'sava's demands if they wished to leave. Maddileh was starting to lean that way too, and the sight of Saralene slowly depleting before her eyes only hardened her resolve.

For her part, Saralene seemed torn in two directions; she wanted to fix the flaws with Findara and couldn't bear the thought of escaping with her life while leaving others in misery. Yet overthrowing Pravhan was clearly a step too far, and she argued against it as much as for it. Who could possibly know the ramifications of such a drastic step?

When dawn came, they were no closer to an answer, but when Penn unbolted the door, it looked as if the decision had been made for them. Four empty guards walked into the tavern, spreading out in front of the trio. Everyone else in the room backed away.

"I think we shall be going to see Pravhan," Mienylyth murmured. "It is, humans, time to make your decision."

EIGHTEEN

Pravhan stood before them rigid and superior. His face betrayed no emotion: not anger at their transgression or triumph at catching them. He might have been stone from the way he appeared so still.

A stiff silence hung between them all; Maddileh shifted uneasily, but a glance from Saralene stilled her. Saralene was an old hand at this game, having played it with her father many times. Silence between opposing parties was to be endured rather than broken by rash statements. Mienylyth sat washing her ears. Saralene had to fight back a smile; dragons, it seemed, were born politicians.

Eventually, Pravhan spoke. "You walked between realms."

"We did," Saralene admitted. What use to deny it now? Pravhan glanced at the Blade.

"I see you bring that foul weapon back into our realm. My brother was a fool to bestow the kiss of Death on it. He should have left well enough alone."

"Many people were saved by his actions," Maddileh snapped.

With a coldness verging on callousness, Pravhan said, "All people die in good time. Why interfere?"

"But death by the Dread Beast was not dying in good time," Saralene said, smooth and reasonable. "It was an early, painful, ignoble death. And it was not in good time. Many young people were slain. Tell me, Prince, who would you have ruled over if all had been slaughtered by the creature? Your realm would have been flooded by the dead initially, but after that . . . ? A trickle. Not enough people would survive to procreate. If you care not about the interests of the living, then you should at least care about your own."

Pravhan smoothed away the ghost of a sneer before he said, "I suppose you thought that because you are not dead or at least not yet fully dead, that you could wander in and out of the Gravelands as you will."

"We thought no such thing, Your Highness," Saralene said respectfully. "We understand that the ability to leave here is entirely at your discretion, but we hope that we might convince you it is to the benefit of the world that we return to continue our work. Maddileh and I—" Saralene knew from his expression that she'd taken the wrong approach even before he cut her off.

"What care I for the world above or your work in it? I care about being defied in my own kingdom. How can I keep order here if women such as you disobey me?"

"What about the stories?" Maddileh said, her tone almost pleading. "Of Otanna, and Speedwell, where you were moved to grant them clemency."

With a chilling smile, Pravhan said, "There is a pit in the palace that I can take you to where you will find Otanna if you want the true story."

Maddileh looked like she'd been slapped in the face.

"Perhaps a trade, then," Mienylyth said. "We have the Resurrection Dish and the Fireborne Blade. Surely either of these would be of interest to a Prince of Death."

"Little dragon," said Pravhan, "I do not bargain life. If

you give me both these things as gifts, I *may* count that in your favour when considering your fate. But I do not *bargain*." His face twisted, as if the word tasted foul.

There was the soft hiss of a sword being drawn from its sheath. Maddileh held the Blade out, pointing it at Pravhan. "A gift, is it? Then take it, Your Highness. Grasp it by the blade and it shall be yours." A flicker of fear ran across Pravhan's face as his eyes fixed on the weapon; then his gaze shifted, and he gave a curt nod. An empty guard stepped in front of her, yanking the sword from her hand just as one stepped behind her, bringing his gauntlet down on the back of her head, so she stumbled to the floor.

"You cannot kill what does not exist," Pravhan said with more than a hint of smugness as the guard handed over the sword, hilt first.

Mienylyth hissed, arching her back ready to spring, but another guard reached down and grabbed her by the scruff of the neck, holding her aloft as she writhed in his grip.

"A poor choice of disguise, dragon," Pravhan said, examining the weapon he held. "Too easily overpowered. Throw them in the labyrinth." He looked at Saralene, and now there was triumph in those cold eyes. "Either time or the ghouls will do for them. Perhaps one, then the other."

As empty gauntlets closed around her arms, Saralene wanted to scream and rage and try to break free, but that would be both impossible and unwise. Even if she managed to escape, she couldn't free either Maddileh or Mienylyth, and she would not leave without them. Instead, she forced down her fear and took careful note of their route so that if—*when*—they escaped the labyrinth, she could find the way out of the castle.

They were hauled down into the depths of the palace. Saralene had expected a door, but instead, they were taken to a circular hole in the ground; runes were carved in the circumference. The guard holding Mienylyth threw her in, Maddileh not far behind. A sharp shove in Saralene's back sent her tumbling over the edge, and as she fell through the gloom towards a distant floor, she felt sure that she would be splattered across the ground on impact. But about twelve feet from the ground, she hit something soft that cushioned her fall so she was gently lowered onto the dirt.

An arrestment spell. Of course. It's no punishment at all if we die on impact.

They were in a wide, open square bordered on each side by high smooth walls. A door stood in each wall, and from what she had glimpsed on the fall downwards, they were at the centre of a complex maze made of the same cold, grey stone walls.

They had been saved from immediate death, but only for a lingering one. As if to emphasise this point, a hideous, hungry cry sounded from the distant darkness.

A stomach-twisting cry jolted Maddileh out of her dazed state and into panicked alertness. The back of her head ached, her pride was severely bruised, and every part of her body was trembling. Now here was a new terror; something else was in this hole with them.

"What do you think that was?" she whispered to Saralene. The mage's skin was hanging loose where the guards had grabbed her, and Maddileh felt a surge of despair nearly sweep her away.

"Don't you remember what the fabric merchant said? Ghouls stalk the passages of the labyrinth. There's only one way out, and nobody has made it yet, because the ghouls track them down and eat them."

Wincing against the pain in her head, Maddileh stood and examined the walls around them. "All right. Let's think of this logically. One way out. I heard once that you can get out of a maze by keeping one hand on the wall, but I don't think we have the time. If I could scale one of these walls, get to the top, then—"

"Foolish humans," Mienylyth snapped. Her ears were flat on her head, and she was staring around, looking hunted. "The fabric merchant said there was only one way out, and logic dictates that if there's one way in, then it must be the only way out too."

Three pairs of eyes looked upwards at the distant hole in the ceiling.

"No," Saralene said, her voice weak. "That's too cruel. He wouldn't."

But Maddileh could too easily imagine it: Pravhan's smugness each time he condemned someone to the labyrinth, offering his subjects the hope of escape through a door that didn't exist, with the real exit unreachable above them. How many souls, she wondered, had looked up at that distant circle of light as they were torn to bits by ghouls, never realising it was what they had been searching for all along?

Trying to not let the impossibility of it all paralyse her mind, Maddileh said, "So, that's our way out. How do we get to it?"

They all stood in silent contemplation for a moment until Mienylyth sighed and stretched out her wings.

"It appears that I am the only one able to do that." She flexed her wings experimentally. "This body is not shaped for flight. Indeed, it should not have wings at all except that I am out of practice at shape-shifting. Perhaps my incompetency will be our salvation."

"Can't you turn back into a dragon and fly us out?" Maddileh asked. Mienylyth gave her a look.

"This underworld is not mine. My magic is bound by the shape I took upon entering. I will not regain my former shape until we leave. I had thought that a sly-eyes walking at your side might be less obvious and therefore more helpful than a sky-rider. If I had known we'd be thrown into an inescapable pit, I might have chosen a different shape," she added caustically.

After an all-over body shudder, Mienylyth crouched down and then leaped upwards, her wings flapping hard and fast. It shouldn't have worked with such short wings and such a dumpy body, but somehow, Mienylyth remained off the ground. The manner was inelegant, and it clearly took immense effort, but the dragon stayed aloft in her cat body. "Wait here," Mienylyth said as she started an unsteady ascent. "And try not to die. Or be killed. Or eaten."

Maddileh watched the creature rise, strangely awestruck. She'd seen dragons in flight before; they were fast, graceful, gliding. Their bones were hollow, it was said, and filled with a gas that gave them extra lift and ensured their long, sinewy bodies could turn as gracefully as a swallow's. Mienylyth's flight was jerky, inelegant, and yet for all that, it was still impressive.

"How do you think she'll be able to help us?" Saralene said, her voice curiously flat.

"I don't know. Get Penn, maybe? But any dragon who—Allfather save us, are you all right?" Maddileh had taken her eyes from Mienylyth's ascent to see that her best friend was swaying where she stood; her skin had a bluish tinge.

"I don't . . . feel . . . well . . ." Saralene said, gently lowering herself to the floor. "I think I'm just tired. A rest will do me good."

Her time's running out, Maddileh thought, the realisation bringing her as close to despair as she'd ever been. *No Blade, no escape, no time.* In the distance came a chittering cry followed by an answering one, then another, fainter and farther away. *And now we're being hunted.*

"Well, *that* I can do something about," she muttered, drawing her sword. Pravhan hadn't ordered the guards to remove that once he had the Blade. She tried to push aside the idea that perhaps he'd left it because he knew it would do her no good.

"I can't defend us here," Maddileh said, helping Saralene to her feet. The mage weighed nothing, and her skin moved unpleasantly under Maddileh's fingertips. "We need our backs against a wall."

After propping Saralene up against one of the walls picked at random, Maddileh examined each doorway and the corridor beyond it. There was no way to block any of the doors, so she'd just have to keep her eye on them all. One corridor led to a junction and a dead end. For a moment, Maddileh thought about moving them there; it was far more defensible than just having their backs against the wall and meant that any attack would be narrowed down to one direction. But the light was weaker, and Maddileh worried that whatever help Mienylyth might bring wouldn't reach them in time if the dragon couldn't find them—or, worse, got attacked looking for them. The most sensible option was to stay where they were, defend themselves as best they could, and wait for whatever help Mienylyth could summon.

When she returned from her investigations, Saralene was sitting up straighter and looked a little brighter, if still very ill. "Find anything useful?"

"Only negatives, but at least that means this is the best course of action," Maddileh said, sitting down next to her friend. "Unless you can conjure up some spell to give us wings so we can fly out of here ourselves."

Saralene gave her a weak smile and patted her pouch. "Damn it, I just used my last wing-growing spell yesterday."

Maddileh grinned.

After a while of sitting in silence, not even hearing the distant cry of ghouls, Saralene suggested they eat something. Not only was Maddileh not hungry, but even if she was, she wouldn't relish the idea of more gravefood. Each meal left her teeth feeling fuzzy. Still, there was nothing else, and her squiring days had taught her that having a bellyful of distasteful food was better than an empty belly. She tried not to watch Saralene nibble on a vegetable pastry that made Maddileh's mouth water. Instead, she forced down sand cake and stale slices of tea bread.

But though the food wasn't to her taste, the company was; she could imagine them back at the High Mage's palace, eating a quiet supper together in Saralene's old rooms, away from the machinations of the court.

"It's almost like old times, isn't it?" Saralene said.

A plaintive wail issued from the depths of the maze.

Even though the sound made her heart stutter, Maddileh forced a smile. "Almost. Needs more onion tarts, though."

To her surprise and delight, Saralene laughed.

"Poor Maddileh. Never had a sweet tooth and now all you've got to eat are cakes." Her face became serious. "I want you to promise me that if the chance comes for you to leave, you'll go, yes? Without me, if necessary."

With resolute patience, Maddileh said, "The whole point of me coming here was to leave again with you. A pretty poor knight I'd be if I left without achieving my objective."

"Yes, but a pretty *alive* knight you'd be as well."

"I'm not leaving without you, Saralene, and that's an end to it. I'm not leaving you. I love you."

The words had been spoken almost without thought, a truth that needed to be said to bolster her argument rather than because the heart demanded it be declared. Just like when she'd kissed Saralene, embarrassment and regret made her both hot and cold.

With a small smile, Saralene reached out and put a hand on top of Maddileh's. "I love you too."

Nineteen

The need to survive was like a burning brand in Saralene's chest. She didn't want to perish here, eaten by ghouls. If she got eaten after her living body died, would that obliterate her soul? What about Maddileh? If her living body was eaten down here, would her soul escape and return to the Perilous Bridge to be judged properly? Too many unknowns.

Time ticked away, unmarked. She didn't even have heart-beats to count. And then she saw them: the ghouls. Figures darting past doorways, always too fast to make out. Then they grew more daring and peered around corners. She saw their empty eye sockets, a dead gaze that pinned her to the spot.

Maddileh tried to chase them away, but whichever door she approached, a ghoul appeared at a different one, creeping forward. Eventually, Maddileh stayed next to Saralene, and they watched the horrors creep across the square towards them. These creatures epitomised the saying "Nothing but skin and bone." There was no flesh on their arms and legs, only papery skin. One or two had evidently been injured, and great rents in their skin revealed old brown bones beneath. There was a void where there should be the healthy bulge of stomach and intestines, and Saralene did not wonder that they were always so hungry. Eyeless, noseless, and hairless, they crept forward.

As Maddileh stood up and hefted her sword, Saralene asked, "You don't have another one of those, do you?" Now she'd seen the fingers of the creatures: brown with dried blood, the finger bones pointed and sharp. Without taking her eyes from the ghouls, Maddileh passed her a dagger.

"That's the best I have, but don't worry. I'll keep them at bay. What else are Champions for?"

"It'd be better if we had fire," Saralene said miserably. "That's the only weapon that works against—"

The ghouls rushed them. Saralene scrambled to her feet, fear banishing exhaustion. The closest ghoul fell to Maddileh's sword, its head hacked off and then its arm. The headless body staggered forward, and Maddileh took the creature's legs out. Still the dismembered limbs twitched, the flat teeth in the head gnashing. The fate of this one seemed to give the others pause, and they backed away, self-preservation momentarily overwhelming hunger. But the open space was filling up with more of them. Three had turned into eight, into fifteen, into twenty-five. Soon, the numbers would be too overwhelming, even for a champion.

What on earth do they live on when there are no humans to punish? Saralene wondered as her gaze scanned the growing horde. Then a movement caught her eye and she saw a rope slither down from the opening above; a feline face peered down at them.

"I have brought salvation," the dragon called.

Maddileh was struggling to cut down two ghouls at once, so Saralene called out, "If you could bring fire too, that would be very helpful."

"Ah, my specialty." Mienylyth launched herself into the air, and while her movements were still a little ungainly, her flight had improved in the time she'd been absent. Gliding over the ghouls at the back, the dragon let out little jets of fire, each short but precisely directed. In a few moments, ghouls were running amok, screaming, and setting alight those around them. Their skin burned fiercely like paper, and their bones smoked.

In the pandemonium, Maddileh and Saralene managed to reach the rope and start to climb. It didn't take long for Maddileh to outstrip Saralene, whose arm muscles were already aching. Glancing back, Maddileh sped up, climbed over the lip, and then hauled on the rope, pulling Saralene up. The mage gripped the rope tightly, her eyes stinging with smoke. Then Maddileh's hands were under her arms, and she scrambled to safety.

They took a few moments to get their breath back before Maddileh urged them to their feet. Saralene couldn't help glancing back down the hole; distant parts of the labyrinth were glowing, lit by blazing ghouls trying to outrun the flames that were gorging on their bones.

"We shouldn't linger," Mienylyth said. "It's not long until sun-death, and that is the only time this ruse will work."

"But how will we find the Prince?" Maddileh asked.

"He won't be far from the Blade, I imagine, and since it was dragon-forged, it calls to me. I can take you to him. The rest is up to you."

The empty guards also proved surprisingly susceptible to dragon fire. "I am definitely taking a dragon with me into every fight," Maddileh said as they watched a guard disintegrate into ash in a matter of seconds.

"Not this sky-rider, though," Mienylyth said. "When we leave here, that will be the last you see of me."

Maddileh was surprised to feel incredibly sad at that statement. However, she didn't have time to dwell on such things as Saralene was getting weaker; they had to rest frequently.

Mienylyth flew up to perch on Maddileh's shoulder and said softly, "Do not despair. I have set plans in place in case your heart-mate succumbs."

"You have?" Maddileh felt her throat tighten with emotion. "Thank you." She coughed and then added, "If we are talking of backup plans, then . . . No mortal blade can harm the Prince, but we've seen that dragon magic—especially dragon fire—has potency here, yes?"

"These things are true."

"And the legends say that only when the Blade is *in Death's hands* can it cut a hole between worlds."

Mienylyth smiled, a grin of daggers. "You have the cold logic of a dragon."

"Thank you. I think."

"This is a good plan, and I will help."

"But only if there is no other way. I don't really want to piss off a Prince of Death if I can avoid it."

For all their efforts to sneak through the palace, Pravhan was waiting for them in his library, seated on a chair behind a desk on which lay the Fireborne Blade.

"You are down numerous ghouls and several guards," Maddileh said as she entered; she walked one way, and Saralene went the other. Pravhan's gaze remained on Maddileh, although no doubt he was watching Saralene from the corner of his eye too.

"So I understand," Pravhan said. "A dragon is a most useful ally, it seems."

When Saralene was at the window, Maddileh said, "Honestly, I would have thought that you, a Prince of—" She made a sudden lunge for the Blade. Pravhan snatched it up and stood in one smooth movement, permitting himself a small smile. He didn't even glance at Saralene, and he certainly didn't see what she had placed on the windowsill.

"Enjoy your elation at escape, knight, because it will be short-lived. There is no place you can run where I can't find you. This is *my* realm and—"

"*Half* your realm," Saralene said, and he glared at her. "You only rule half. Your brother has the other."

"Is that your plan? To run to his realm and hide? I have servants who can follow and—"

"Look," Saralene said, gesturing behind her. "The sun has set." Pravhan's eyes flicked to the window and then down at himself.

"But . . . I . . . How?"

"A sunstone," Saralene said, now pointing to the glowing orb on the windowsill that cast daylight into the room as if it naturally fell through the window. "Night and day at the same time."

As the horror of this realisation crossed Pravhan's face, the air around him blurred, like a heat haze, and C'sava sidestepped into existence out of the same space Pravhan had been occupying. The twins locked gazes, C'sava smiling with easy confidence, Pravhan gaping.

C'sava's hand snaked out, stabbing a jeweled dagger into his brother's arm. Pravhan howled in pain, his hand convulsively letting go of the Blade, which C'sava caught with deft grace. He angled the weapon and then thrust it forward, embedding it in Pravhan's chest. As his brother's eyes widened with shock, C'sava leaned forward and whispered, "This is the second time I've watched you die. And for what it's worth, this time, I'm truly sorry."

A cascade of grey ash fell from Pravhan's mouth, washing away any last words he might have spoken. He sank, lifeless, to the floor.

As C'sava cleaned the blade, Maddileh hurried over to Saralene, who was slouching against the windowsill. "It's important," Maddileh whispered as she drew her upright, "that you watch what he does." Turning to C'sava, she said, "You have the Blade and the kingdom; now cut a way between worlds, as you promised."

After a brief hesitation, C'sava shrugged and used the tip of the Blade to draw a sigil in the air around which he carved a circle. When the circle was complete, the fabric of the Gravelands fell away, and the blue sky of the living world was visible. Maddileh started to help Saralene towards the doorway, but C'sava stepped in front of it, smiling and counting down. "Three, two, one."

Saralene slumped in Maddileh's arm, her skin sliding off her. "No!" Maddileh cried. Behind C'sava, the way was shrinking, closing.

A new, dead Saralene opened her eyes, blinking hard. "Go," she whispered. "While you still can."

"No," Maddileh said firmly. Her gaze shifted to Mienylyth, who had placed her paws on Saralene's chest. The dragon breathed onto the serpentstone necklace, words of power mingling with her exhalation.

"No!" This time it was C'sava crying out. "Stop! I do not permit this!"

Saralene's eyes were fluttering as a golden glow from the stone wrapped tendrils around her. She murmured something, and then the tendrils slipped inside her mouth, sliding down her throat, and suddenly, her whole body was a blaze of light. Maddileh squeezed her eyes shut against such a glare, and when she opened them again, Saralene lay there whole and healthy. The skin she had shed was mere dust on the floor.

As Maddileh helped her friend to her feet, C'sava glared at them. "It matters not." He glanced over his shoulder; the way between worlds was almost gone. "You are trapped here, and I merely have to wait until your bodies succumb to death again."

"You promised you'd release us," Maddileh said.

With a cold, cruel smile, he said, "There's only one type of release Death can give you, knight. My brother was wrong about many things, but he was right that defying death is an insult to the ruler of the Gravelands that cannot be tolerated. You were never going to leave this place except at the end of the Blade. When time here has taken your lives from you, the Blade will give your soul its ultimate release, and you will be obliterated."

With a yell of fury, Maddileh drew her sword and charged. C'sava raised the Blade defensively. "No mortal blade can harm me," he said, laughing, as the ferocity of Maddileh's attack forced him backward. She pinned him to the wall, her blade at his throat; his grin was insufferable.

"I know. That wasn't what I was planning at all," she snarled.

There was a flash of light and C'sava screamed in agony as dragon fire burned through his wrist, severing his hand, still holding the sword. Maddileh snatched up both and gave them to Saralene, who looked sickened. "Death's hand," Maddileh urged. "Use it to draw the same sigil he did."

With a grim expression, Saralene gripped the severed limb and repeated C'sava's actions, so that a way opened before them. Maddileh felt claws dig into her shoulder as Mienylyth leaped up and held on, and then she was diving through the opening, pulling Saralene with her, C'sava screaming curses behind them.

Once through the portal, Maddileh felt only momentary relief before the severity of their situation made itself plain. In an ultimate act of treachery, C'sava had opened a way back into the living world several miles above the ground. He hadn't intended for them to survive, even if they made it through the opening.

Maddileh still had hold of Saralene's hand, and the two of them grasped each other tighter, ensuring the wind didn't wrench them apart. Maddileh watched the ground racing towards her, feeling more cheated than afraid. They'd come so far, and now they would meet their deaths anyway. It didn't seem fair.

And then something wrapped around her waist, tugging her sideways, and she was no longer falling but gliding. She looked up at Mienylyth's scaled underbelly and then to the left, where Saralene was securely held in the dragon's other claw.

Mienylyth twisted her long neck down to look at them

both, her reptilian gums pulled back into a wide smile. "Caught you."

The noise that came from Maddileh's mouth had no words; it was the sound of pure joy. They were alive and flying like dragons.

TWENTY

Once Saralene had learned that the purpose of the palace's high ceilings was to ensure dragons could fit beneath, she knew she'd never be able to look up again and not feel a pang of regret at what might have been. How much greater would their knowledge of magic and the world be with a council of dragons to aid them? Or even just Mienylyth's wisdom? But the dragon could not be pressed to stay any longer than it took to ensure the emperor gave his agreement that dragons would no longer be hunted.

She would never forget the sight of the finest nobles and knights in the land backing away from her and Maddileh as they walked the length of the emperor's Great Hall with a dragon behind them. After a weaving of her own blood magic had been distilled into the air around them, Saralene had ensured that all present had been able to hear Mienylyth's voice—temporarily at least.

"Bowing your head to the emperor was a nice touch," Maddileh had said afterwards. "Convinced them of your sincerity."

With a dragon's black humour, Mienylyth replied, "It is no great thing to make a meaningless bow to a creature you could obliterate with a snap of your jaws."

Now the sun was setting, and the three of them were

standing on the balcony of the High Mage's apartments, Mienylyth's scales reflecting the burnished gold of the sky.

"Where will you go?" Maddileh asked.

"Towards the horizon," Mienylyth answered softly. "After that, I do not know. I will seek out others as I fly, see if they will join me. The blood of the noble dragons is much diminished these days, but perhaps there are still some I could call companion." With a great sigh, she swung her head round to look at the two women. "I have lived long and alone. Likely I will live longer and grow lonelier still. A heart-mate is not something to be lightly discarded. You should not let politics or station, custom, or even death prevent a blending of souls. Remember that. Perhaps we shall meet again. I trust you will not take it amiss if I say I hope we do not. May Voice bless you."

As Mienylyth opened her wings, beating them in one great stroke that sent the two women staggering in the downdraft, a small voice in Saralene's head whispered back, *May Voice guide you.* They were not her words, but they felt right.

As Mienylyth flew away, Saralene and Maddileh watched her go, standing so close they were almost touching. "Honestly, dragons are such high-and-mighty know-it-alls," Maddileh said.

"Perhaps. But she was right." Putting a hand on either cheek, Saralene pulled Maddileh forward and kissed her, gently at first and then with an intensity born of longing.

This time, the kiss was exactly as Saralene had imagined it would be.

Once they had parted, Saralene rested her head on Maddileh's chest. She thought of Luciel's timeless vigil, of an afterlife with no animals, and, most of all, the loneliness of dragons. As Mienylyth's great form diminished into nothing, Saralene knew how lucky she was to be in her lover's arms, watching the sunset, with life stretching before her. She swore she would not waste even a moment of it.

Acknowledgments

After writing the acknowledgments for *The Fireborne Blade*, I was worried I wouldn't have enough thanks to put in the acknowledgments section of book two, but it turns out that everyone has been awesome in new ways (and also that I know super amazing people who just continue to be awesome in general).

Once again, first and greatest thanks to my amazing Tordotcom team. Lee Harris continues to keep an eye on the words, and Matt Rusin keeps me on the straight and narrow (as best anyone can). Michael Dudding, Alexis Saarela, and Samantha Friedlander—oh my god, you guys have been amazing with all the work you've put into marketing *The Fireborne Blade*. I feel overwhelmed by your faith and humbled by your expertise. A special thank-you to Amy Sefton for the dragon stats cards—what a cool thing to create!

I got my lovely copy editor back, although Sara Robb didn't laugh at as many of my jokes as last time (note to try harder in future books). Thanks also to my proofreader, Shawna Hampton, and cold reader, Marcell Rosenblatt, for picking up all the bits I missed.

Huge thanks to Martina Fačková and Christine Foltzer for another stunning cover—and look at the dragon cat! After seeing her rendered so beautifully, I really hope I'm allowed to write another novella wholly about the dragon cat. . . .

A shout-out definitely has to be given to all those people who invited me to speak in person or on paper about *The Fireborne Blade* when it was released. It was such a thrill to find people genuinely excited about my book—you guys really gave me a boost! Thank you so much for reaching out, and I hope you like book two as much.

Alex Cochran continues to be my rock, helping me to make sense of a brand-new world.

Huge thanks to Megan Leigh, Lucy Hounsom, and Sarah Deeming, in particular, for being so enthusiastic about *The Fireborne Blade* and making me feel less nervous about sending it out into the world.

My regular meet-ups with Andy Knighton, Adrian Tchaikovsky, and Tim Major always provide highlights in a career that can be a touch lonely. In a similar vein, Priya Sharma, Penny Jones, and Shona Kinsella continue to be amazing at cheering me up when I need it most.

Jane Skudder, Helen Vaughan, and Jane Holburn need to get a mention for being the bestest friends ever.

Thanks always, Raphael, who always believes in me.

Talking of people who believed in me, in those formative years at school, there were three teachers in particular who guided and inspired me, and I was negligent not to thank them in my previous book. Mr. Heselton—thank you for encouraging a girl to put pen to paper and create everything from satire to vampires; I wouldn't have a book now if I hadn't started out scribbling in your class. Mr. Brettell— the methodical attitude and appreciation for the nuances of language that you instilled into our Latin lessons are put to good use every day; I still smile whenever I come across Latin in my daily life. Mr. Temple—your enthusiasm for science helped me to develop an enquiring mind and find the joy of solving puzzles; every writer starts with "what if . . . ?"

And, as ever, thanks to my husband and daughter, who are just my world. (And I should probably mention the cats at this point, too, who provide entertainment, affection, and numerous typos when they walk on the keyboard.)

About the Author

Kate Maxwell

CHARLOTTE BOND is an author, freelance editor, and podcaster. Under her own name, she has written within the genres of horror and dark fantasy, but she's also worked as a ghostwriter. She edits books for individuals and publishers, and has also contributed numerous nonfiction articles to various websites. She is a cohost of the award-winning podcast *Breaking the Glass Slipper*. Her microcollection, *The Watcher in the Woods*, won the British Fantasy Society Award for Best Collection in 2021.